THE MARY B CHRONICLES

THE LONG WAY AROUND BOOK 3

DAKIARA

MIND FLOW PUBLISHING & PRODUCTION LLC PRESENTS

First Printing: 2020

ISBN 978-1-951271-06-0 Paperback

ISBN 978-1-951271-07-7 Ebook

Additional copies of this book and others are available by mail or by visiting the website listed below. Check website for pricing.

Mind Flow Publishing & Production LLC

PO Box 48768 Cumberland, North Carolina 28331-8768

www.mindflowpublishingproduction.com

Cover design by Carrie & Co.

Editing by Stories Matter Editing

Formatting Design by Covers My Way

Thank you for helping to bring Mary B to Life......

DEDICATED TO MY LOVES

DAQUAN, DEJA, DANTE

KEVONN AND KIARA

RIP
DAQUAN JAMIQUE 95
&
KIARA DENISE 00

Special Thanks
To GOD for Giving Me
The Strength and The Words
To Do This Project.
Blessed by The Experiences to Draw From
It Has Not Always Been Easy.

Dedicated to Some Who Have Gone Before Me
Mary Merriman
Naomi Thompson

PROLOGUE

Robert was feeling encouraged with Davina and her progress, she was determined. He loved seeing her passion for walking again. She had lost hope on more than one occasion. That was something he didn't want to see too often. They had been through a lot and overcame it. He was thankful that they fought their way through and back to each other. Their house had never been happier. The only concern that he could honestly say he had was when he caught Janet starring at him a few times too many. He didn't say anything to Davina about it because she was working hard, and he didn't want to disrupt that. He told himself he would keep an eye on it to see if it continued.

CHAPTER ONE

OVER THE LAST FEW DAYS WILLIAM HAD BEEN WORKING up his nerve to ask Christian for a favor. He still had the strands of hair that he had brushed from Janet's jacket just days earlier when they first met at Robert's house. William had also taken some from Robert's brush. He felt so shady doing it, but he wanted to get them tested to see if there was any way possible that they were related. He just had to be sure.

It's crazy that he had been sure for so many years that he didn't have any other children but now that Janet was older, he wasn't so sure. There were certain characteristics that made him question it, like her eyes and hair, although in that area things like that were not that uncommon. If it were true, he knew Mary would be hurt, but he had to know. He knew he couldn't live with that secret.

William had thought to ask Tim for help, but he didn't want him to get caught up in anything crazy. He felt like Christian was more on his level and would understand; at least he hoped he would. William asked Christian to hang out and play pool, and then he hit him with his plan.

"Hey Christian, man I need a favor, and I wouldn't ask but it is kind of important."

"You sound serious Will, what's going on? Whatever you need man, anything I have is yours you should know that. Your family has been amazing throughout this whole ordeal. Name it, and it's yours."

"I guess I need to explain a little bit first, that only seems right," Taking a deep breath, William begins his tale. "I will try and make this as short a story as possible, I promise. Before I met Mary B, I used to be with this woman named Phyllis. We were together for two years and when we broke up, shortly thereafter she had a baby. It was a baby girl that she named Janet."

Christian's eyebrow rose slightly, like he was making the connection.

"Yeah, yeah, I knew there would be no judgment coming from you my friend. Yes, it is the same one who is doing therapy with Davina. Anyway, I was very certain that she wasn't mine, but there are a few similarities that I can't seem to shake. So, I just want to make sure, I've always told Mary B that Phyllis assured me that there was no possible way that she was mine. I did help take care of her for some years financially, but nothing else. Phyllis fooled around on me a few times and so I ended up breaking it off with her. She had too much going, and I didn't want any part of it. So, my question is, can you help me? The only thing is you can't tell anyone."

"That's a lot to take in, but I do understand the situation. I'd be a hypocrite if I said I didn't. I wasn't due to go back to work for another week or so, but if we can get some DNA, then we can get the test run. It takes no time at all. So, let me know when you've got some sort of DNA that we can test." Christian said, nodding at William.

William reached into his jacket and pulled out his bags with the hair samples that he had taken from Robert and Janet and handed them over.

"Are you serious right now man? How do you just happen to have hair samples in a bag in your jacket pocket? I guess you really need to know. What are you going to do with this information once you get it, are you going to break Mary B's heart? I've learned a lot over the last few months about this family, and trust ranks pretty high on the list of things not to violate. What about your children? What will they think or say?"

William looked horrified for a moment as it finally sunk in what was about to happen and the repercussions it could have on everyone close to him. How would he tell Mary B? What about the kids? For a moment he thought he was being selfish. He had been standing with his arms crossed they dropped as he began to talk.

"I'm not trying to wreck my home. It's more so that I know one way or another. The feeling of not knowing is really getting to me. I don't really know what I'd do with the information. But I can't imagine having a kid and not being there for them. I value my family above all else."

Christian could sense William's anxiety was rising. He didn't like the apprehensive look on his face. Christian knew it was important to him to find out, so at that moment he made a promise to himself to help out however he could.

"Okay Will, I will get the test done tomorrow first thing.

I will warn you, sometimes knowing is worse than not knowing. I don't regret Kevin, but if I hadn't pushed so hard then so many things wouldn't have happened. Look at Davina, she is still struggling to get back to normal. She may eventually have to tell a set of twins, 'hey you two have different dads.' That's nothing to have to tell children. If it weren't for me pushing to find out, because I selfishly wanted closure, it wouldn't even be an issue."

Christian had been standing directly across from William during their intense conversation but once he began talking, he began pacing back and forth, shaking his head at the thoughts of the recent past crashed over him. He wanted to shake some sense into William, to not to go down this road, and just let it be, but he knew his friend was past the point of no return.

"It wasn't all bad though, if you hadn't pushed for that knowledge, they wouldn't know that Kevin has kidney disease, and it could have been detrimental to his health. I'd much rather know that he has those issues early on, even though it came with you. You're not half bad,"

"I already told you I would do your test. You don't have to try and butter me up." Christian chuckled.

William was thankful for his friend. Grinning he slapped Christian on his back and pulled him into a hug.

"Thanks man, you have no idea how much this is weighing on me."

"No problem, usually we can get results within a few days unless the lab is backed up. I will use the utmost discretion. That goes without saying. As soon as I get the results, I will let you know." With that the two gentlemen parted ways for the evening.

William trusted Christian to keep his secret. He knew it was a lot to ask of anyone, especially someone who was trying to reconnect with his own family, but William felt he didn't have any other viable options. He just kept praying that she wasn't his child. If it came out that way, he couldn't even imagine how much of a strain it would put on his marriage and it could do quite a bit of damage to his children as well.

———

MARY B'S MIND HAD BEEN WORKING OVERTIME SINCE she laid eyes on Janet. She couldn't put her finger on it but there was something familiar about her. Those eyes and hair were unmistakable, but it wasn't that uncommon in that area. The town they lived in and the surrounding area was known to have a mixture of people. It was rare in most cases to find someone who wasn't of mixed race.

Mary B liked that about her town because that was one less thing that she had to worry about. Racism was pretty much nonexistent. But knowing that didn't make Mary B's mind settle down. She was determined to figure it out.

———

WHEN CHRISTIAN LEFT WILLIAM, HE DID SOMETHING he hadn't done in a while, he went to the nearby bar and got a drink. This family had been through so much, and he feared that there were still more trials to come. He didn't mind doing the favor for Will; he just wanted him to be sure that he indeed wanted to know what the results could mean, and what impact that knowledge could have on his life. He had one drink just to take his mind off of things and he headed home.

When he got home Tim was waiting up. He was a bit concerned because Mary B had called and said her package had made it home okay. That was part of their game, to make sure everyone was safe and sound. Tim could smell the cigarettes and he smelled the beer on his dad's breath. He was concerned and asked if he was okay. Christian told him that he had stopped off at the bar and that it was only one drink, just to get some things off his mind. He told him that he hadn't gone back to his drinking and partying ways. He had too much at stake and too much to live for these days to ever go back to that kind of lifestyle.

Tim was a little worried about his dad. He was still on his medication to lessen the chance of having another epileptic seizure and alcohol use did affect the way the medicine performed. He also remembered that his dad had started drinking a lot right before he left him and his mom. He didn't want to pressure him too much, but he wanted him to let him know he cared just the same. Tim knew that Christian was thinking he was wearing out his welcome, he had mentioned to Jean, to see if she had a problem with him staying indefinitely. Jean told him no, they had plenty of room and the children loved having him there. "As long as he helps us out around here then its fine. I think it's good that he is here, for you and him." Tim didn't want to let on that he was concerned about his drinking, because he knew she would overreact, and he didn't want that.

He decided he would trust Christian and pray it was as he said. Tim promised himself he would speak with Christian at some point within the next few days and see what his plans were as far as living arrangements go.

As promised, Christian took the hair samples with him to the hospital the next morning. He knew a lot of the techs that worked in the lab, so they didn't mind doing this favor for him. He asked Bruce to use the utmost discretion, and that no one was to know the results except him. He agreed and began processing the samples. Bruce assured Christian that he would get the results back to him as soon as he could. Christian slipped Bruce a fifty-dollar bill for his assistance. Bruce hands it back to him and tells him that that is not necessary. He joked and said he was bored anyway; and needed something to do to occupy his time. Bruce felt bad for earning a paycheck and not producing any work. Christian thanked him and left him to it, after he gave him his cell phone number.

He just so happened to be looking at his phone at the exact moment William was calling. "Hey Chris, sorry to bother you man, but was just checking to make sure you were able to drop that thing off?"

"Yeah man, it's taken care of. Let me call you later, I'm in the lab at the hospital right now. I'll call you as soon as I know something." William murmured a quick goodbye and hung up.

Christian thought to himself, *this man is going to drive himself crazy.* He just hoped the results came back the way they needed to. He was enjoying the peace that seemed to be over the family now. That reminded him, he needed to talk to Tim and Jean about whether he would be staying with them or not. He headed from the lab and went back to his office to finish up some paperwork before heading out for the night.

AFTER A MONTH OF THERAPY, DAVINA WAS READY TO show everyone the progress she had made. She was beyond proud of herself that she was finally able to ambulate over forty feet. Davina was determined that by the time Jean had her baby girl that she would be able to walk in and out of the hospital with limited use of a cane. She was thankful that she was paired up with Janet. She pushed her awfully hard during their therapy sessions, but it was worth it. Even though at the end of some of the sessions she had vowed to fire Janet, she even went so far as telling her that she hated her once.

Janet simply said, "Good, then I am definitely doing my job then. I told you that might happen. We still have a long way to go though, so just don't give up on me." Usually at the end of each session Janet would say "Don't give up on me," Davina promised not to.

The best part was that Robert didn't know how far she had come, since most of her sessions had taken place while he was at work. She looked forward to seeing the look on his face when she showed him as well. That day she was going to make sure Mary B could watch the children. She had been planning a long time for this night for Robert; she had to make up for lost time. He would finally have his wife back completely. Even though he never complained she knew he missed having her physically, as well as mentally.

AFTER THE FENDER BENDER, JEAN HAD BEEN TAKING IT easy. She had Tim home so she was milking it for all she could. He was more than accommodating, he had indeed missed being with the family.

"Hey baby, did you ever get in touch with Bianca?" Jean mentioned one night while they were relaxing at home.

"I called her and left a few messages, but I haven't received a call back. I had almost forgot about it to be honest," Tim hadn't quite forgotten about it, but he didn't want to worry his wife. He was hoping that it was just a coincidence. The fact remained that they had the paperwork saying all parental rights were theirs, and no father was listed on the birth certificate, and to further seal the deal, it was notarized. He fervently hoped that nothing would come of it.

This pregnancy had been taking its toll on Jean, she was determined that this had to be the last baby. She didn't think her body could handle the demands another pregnancy would take on her body. She hoped that Tim was going to be okay with that fact. He noticed that she seemed more stressed than normal, and he wondered if they had taken on too much with taking Kim in. Jean was tired all the time, and he didn't like it. That wasn't his Jeannie.

Over dinner one night when she was close to four months along, Tim asked if she was really okay with everything.

"Yes, I'm fine. I'm just tired. These two little ones, the one on the outside and this one trying to break free are wearing me out. You would think I would be able to handle it with ease, since we did just have a set of twins. At my last checkup everything was good; all my levels were where they should be. Would you be mad if we didn't have any more after this?" Tim couldn't shake his head fast enough.

"We are good baby. I love my family as is. If we were blessed with another, then I guess that was part of God's plan, but I am good. You've given me so much more than I have ever dared to hope for. I know it is wearing you out and for that I am sorry, I promise if I could take all of it away from you and carry that weight myself trust me I would."

There were many times in their lives together that she was just in amazement of her husband, and this was one of them. She loved him more than life itself and she would always do what she could to show him that. Tim pulled her into his embrace and told her to prop up her feet; he saw that they were swollen.

Although she was gorgeous blossoming with his child, he hated that she was going through so much. He truly couldn't imagine carrying a child while also carrying for another, especially when they were less than a year apart. She did it with grace and love. He loved her for her sacrifices for their family. Miles and Dayshaun didn't always make it easy for her, if there were something to get into, they were in it, but school wise they were on top of it. He was grateful for that.

CHAPTER TWO

WITHIN A WEEK, BRUCE CALLED CHRISTIAN TO LET HIM know that the test results were in. Christian was there in record time, he resisted peeking since that wasn't his place. He felt that if William wanted to share the results he would. Besides if he knew, that might complicate his relationship with the family. Before he left the parking garage, he was on the phone with William.

"Hey man, I have that thing for you." Christian said as soon as William answered the phone.

"I wasn't trying to get on your nerves man but thank you for taking care of it. Well, don't keep me in suspense what did it say?"

"I don't know, I didn't look at them, I didn't think it was my place to. That is your business, I'm just an honorary member of the family." William chuckled through the phone.

"I will catch up with you later; Mary B has some errands to run. I think we are supposed to end up over at Jean and

Tim's place anyway." Christian told him that was fine. He would just see him when they got there.

William's nerves had been a tumultuous mess since he asked Christian for that favor. He kept replaying everything that happened over and over in his mind. For William to be such a calm and collected man, he was about to find out something that could turn his well-ordered world upside down, and that had him all beside himself. He was anxious to get the errands handled so he could hurry and get to Jean's.

In all of his rushing around he became more and more agitated, he even yelled at Mary B. He said she was taking too long to do nothing. Mary B raised her eyebrow and said, "What in the world is wrong with you? You have never talked to me like that. Something has been brewing with you for a minute now, so you might as well go ahead and spill it." He immediately felt bad, because she was right, he was out of his mind right now, and had been for a while, and he was being unfair to her. He wasn't ready to tell her what was going on just yet though.

"Mary B just bear with me; I promise I will tell you what's going on as soon as I know. Okay? Can you please just trust me?" Mary B had always trusted him so there was no reason to stop now. She couldn't resist pushing his buttons though, just to keep him on his toes.

"I trust you William, but if you are cheating on me, so help me, God himself won't be able to save you from what I will have in store for you."

William's eyes got super wide, and he knew that she was not joking. He let out a sigh, "Please Mary B, stop it with that foolish talk right now. Why must you always threaten me? I haven't done nothing woman,"

Although Mary believed him, she still had an inkling that he was hiding something. She would wait it out, but if he didn't spill his guts soon, she was going to have him sleeping on the couch, and she knew how much he hated that.

After they finished up the errands they couldn't get to Jean's fast enough. Christian's car wasn't there when they arrived, but he was determined not to panic. He knew he couldn't give Mary B any more ammunition to fire her shots with. He knew she would bring it up when he least expected it. Jean opened the door looking tired, and Mary B began fussing over her. William was thankful for that distraction, no matter how long it might last. He was just thankful for the break from Mary B's intense scrutiny.

Tim wasn't home either, so William went into the living room and turned on the TV and sank into the couch. As soon as he got comfortable though in burst Miles and Dayshaun, "Grandpa, Grandpa,"

William pretended he had fallen asleep, but they didn't buy it. One grabbed his arm and the other jumped on his leg. "Oh, hey boys, what's going on?" He asked with a smile. Miles spoke up, "Nothing much Grandpa. Will you play catch with us? Dad's not here, and Mom isn't able to."

Just then the door opens and in walks Christian, William was saved, he hated to have to tell the boys no. "Hey Chris, it's good to see you. You don't know just how much." William's face lit up when he saw Christian. "Yeah you too Will. That reminds me I have something for you in the car. You mind stepping outside?"

William got up and apologized to the boys and said he would be back in a bit. Once outside they got into Christian's car, and he handed him the envelope. Christian asked him again, "Are you sure that you want to open that? Once you do there is no turning back. Some things can't be undone." William reached for it and shook his head yes. He knew Christian was only trying to keep him from making a mistake, but he felt he had to know. Opening the envelope, he took in a deep breath, and pulled the papers from the inside. He didn't really know what it was that he was looking at, so he handed them to Christian. "Please, tell me what they say," William asked.

As Christian glanced over the paperwork, he looked confused. "I thought you said you were possibly the girl's father?" William nodded; Christian looked again at the papers. "To make a long story very short, you are not the father."

William didn't like the way Christian hesitated, "Seems like there is more going on there?"

"Paternally there is no match, but maternally there are a lot of similarities, enough in fact to give the impression that Mary B and Phyllis are related, perhaps even sisters. Is that possible?"

William's jaw dropped that was not what he was expecting at all. Mary B had never mentioned having a sister, or any siblings for that matter. He only remembered her saying something about some cousins. She had never been very talkative when it came to her family. He knew it wasn't the best experience growing up for her.

"Wow, Mary has a sister? I wonder if she knows. What if Phyllis knew the whole time?" So many questions flooded his mind. *Oh, my goodness, what was he going to tell Mary B? How was he going to tell her?*

Christian seen the wheels in his mind turning. "Man, I told you sometimes you don't always need to know. Yeah, I know I'm one to talk, but still. Thankfully, things for me didn't turn out too bad." As he said that he avoided looking at William. Reluctantly the men got out of the car and made their way into the house. William was walking as if he was in a trance and Christian had to steady him. They made it to the couch, William just kept shaking his head. Christian was reassuring him, that it was going to be okay.

Just then Mary B, and Jean, came into the room. The ladies could tell that they had walked in on something pretty serious. William and Christian stopped dead in their tracks, like deer caught in the headlights. "Alright William, what is it? What in the world is going on? You've been whispering with Christian non-stop for the last week or so."

Taking a deep breath, William gathered his thoughts and told her what he did and why he did it. He even told her that he wished he hadn't.

"Mary B don't be mad. I know how you get, but I couldn't help myself, I needed to know the truth." Mary B was looking a little confused as her gaze ping-ponged between Christian and William.

"Spit it out William,"

"Well, you remember before we got together, I was with Phyllis, right? You also recall her having a little girl not long after we broke up?" Mary B was nodding her head. "Well that little girl is Janet, the one who is doing therapy with Davina. I hadn't thought about her in years, but as she has gotten older, I couldn't help but think there was a slight resemblance to Robert and Jean. Well I asked Christian if he would do a DNA test for me and he did. Stop looking at him like that; he was just doing me a favor, woman. The results were conclusive, I am not her father." He paused to take a deep breath, and Mary B looked at him expectantly to continue his tale.

"Maybe we should talk alone?" he said quietly, as he took in the stunned expression that everyone in the room seemed to be wearing.

"William, if you don't spit it out already."

"Mary B, you are more stubborn than the devil himself. Do you have any siblings? Before you go getting defensive and all, the test showed that Robert and Janet are related, on the maternal side. That would be you. You didn't have another child that I don't know about do you?" If looks could kill, William would have been six feet under.

Mary B stared a hole in his head. "No, there was no other child William, I'd have told you if there were, better yet, the child would have been with me. When I was growing up, someone slipped up once and told me I had a sister. My momma denied it, and said they were crazy. I grew up with just my cousins; they were my sisters and brothers. I never would have lied to you about something like that. You of all people know what family means to me. Is there a chance your test was wrong Christian?" But Christian sadly shook his head no.

Mary B's world had suddenly shifted on its axis. So many questions clouded her mind. Why would her mom have kept that from her? She had a sister? There was only one person who was still alive in her family that might know what the truth was. She had an uncle whose name was

Theodore, but they called him Teddy for short. He was getting up there in age and she wasn't sure if he would remember what happened or even tell her, but he had nothing more to hide or lose.

"William, I'm not sure of anything anymore. I am more confused than I have ever been in my life. I need to go see Teddy right now, can you take me? He is the only one who knows the truth. All these years I've been alone and come to find out perhaps I didn't have to be."

William was almost in tears at the look on her face, how dare he bring her to this place of confusion. Their life was just fine as it was, but he was selfish and just had to know. He couldn't just leave well enough alone. Just as he reached out to grab Mary B's hand, her knees buckled beneath her, but he caught her as he always did.

William was her protector and the solid presence in her life, and he felt as if he had failed her for the first time since they had begun their journey together.

This whole time as William and Mary B were having this conversation, Christian, Tim, and Jean were sitting in shocked silence. No one knew what to say to ease the tension that had descended upon the room. This was the first time that Jean had seen her mom in this state of mind. Her mom was always strong and full of life, sure of her convictions. She knew she needed to call Robert, and that they needed to be together. She thought to herself that she had never heard her mom talk about an Uncle Teddy. It just seems like one secret after another was unraveling there in the living room.

Picking up the phone she dials Robert's number. He answered on the first ring and Jean asks him if he could come to her house as soon as possible. Within thirty minutes he is standing at the door.

"What's going on Jean? Is my mom okay?" He asked because he saw his dad holding onto her for dear life. He was shaken by seeing his mom in this state as well. For the next hour they began talking about the events that led up until this moment. One thing they were sure of is that they would figure it out. They always did and they would do it together.

William agreed that he would take Mary B to see this uncle of hers tomorrow. Robert and Jean said they wanted to go too. They looked at their mom for her to say it was okay. At that moment it was like they were kids again, awaiting her approval. She nodded yes without hesitation.

"I am sorry you both are seeing me this way. I don't know what he may say, or even if he will tell the truth after all this time. All I can do is ask him for the truth. William, you have to know that no matter what, I'm not upset that you did this behind my back, although I do wish you would have just told me. What hurts now is that I have so many questions that are unanswered."

"We will go first thing in the morning. Christian, I know I'm all out of favors, but could you perhaps watch the kids? It shouldn't take too long, it's an hour drive there and back. I promise we will get back as quickly as possible. Can you do that for me?"

"I think I've caused enough trouble, so I dare not say no. I'd be happy to watch them. I truly hope that you get the answers you need and deserve. And for the record, I'm sorry for bringing extra stress on your family. That was never my intention." Christian said in a heartfelt tone.

"We know, and it is okay, there is no one at fault here.

We are family." The words were heartfelt as they spilled from Mary B's lips. They all agreed that they should all get some sleep and decided to leave by 9 a.m. As eager as she was for answers, she was equal amounts of anxious and nervous. She had no idea what she would find out. With William and the kids by her side she knew it would be okay.

"What about the child? Should we tell her what we know as of now, or wait until we have more to tell?" Mary B asked, as she looked at the faces of those she loved most.

"Momma let's wait until we know more. There is no need to disrupt her life. Who knows she may already know. We will just wait and see what happens first."

CHAPTER THREE

BIANCA FINALLY RETURNED JEAN'S CALL AS THEY WERE on their way to Uncle Teddy's. As badly as Jean wanted to talk to her, to find out what was going on, she knew she needed to be there for her mother at that moment.

"Bianca now is not a good time. I just need to know, is everything okay? I had left several messages and didn't hear back, so I began to worry." Jean murmured into the phone.

"Everything is okay. Lucas is home, he surprised me by coming home early."

"Was he in an accident when he first got back? I think we met him. I knew that wouldn't be the best way to meet him and introduce ourselves. I was getting paranoid because I thought it was on purpose. So much has been going on, my mind was running wild. What if he didn't want to give the baby up and he wanted to take us out of the picture. Maybe he thought we approached you about your child."

"Yes, he was in an accident, he showed me the paper with your name on it, and explained to me what happened. That's another reason why I'm calling. I know I said I wasn't going to tell him the truth, but I realized that even though I felt like it was and still is the right thing for you to raise Kim, I didn't give him that choice. When he told me about the accident, I felt it was fated that I be honest with him. So, we went away and spent a few days at the beach, and we had a heart to heart. Once I told him, he of course said he hated me, but then he held me close and said he loved me more. He was thankful that I told him, he said the one request he had was that he meet you. He couldn't believe I trusted you so much as to feel as if you were a fit mother for our child, but I couldn't stop going on about you. He is fine with her being with you and us being far into the background, he just wants to be sure too."

Jean just listened and told her that once she was able to get some business handled that she would call her back to set up a meeting. Jean was proud of Bianca for doing the right thing. Right now, she couldn't focus, there was too much going on, but Jean knew that all would be okay in the end.

Uncle Teddy was residing at Shady Acres Nursing Home; Jean was surprised to find out as they pulled up to the building. Teddy was Mary's mother's last living brother, her last living relative. Mary B was slow getting out of the car, she was a ball of nerves, but she knew she must go forward. William walked to her side and grabbed her hand and kissed it. He whispered that he loved her. She smiled; she loved him more than life itself.

Robert and Jean walked behind their parents. The two of them didn't know what to expect, they were thinking he was some old creepy man. They weren't far from the truth. When they asked for Theodore, they were instructed to wait in the sitting area and they would bring him out in just a few.

They seemed surprised that he had visitors; during his tenure at the home there was only one other time had he had one. That was the day his wife left him, after she signed him in. She came the next day to drop off his belongings and asked him to sign the divorce papers.

When they brought him into the sitting area, he was a frail husk of a man. Nothing like the man Mary B remembered. He stood there looking at her for a minute. A smile crept to his face, "Mary is that you? You are as beautiful as ever," he said as he adjusted his glasses. He looked around at everyone that was there. "Why are you here? No one has been to visit me, well since I've been here."

"Uncle Teddy, I don't have many memories of you and my mother for that matter, but I have a question to ask. I need you to be honest with me. Can you do that?" Teddy shook his head affirmatively, "I will try to answer it the best I can. What is it"? Mary grabbed William's hand again and held it tight. "What is it Mary? Why are you acting as if you're scared of me or of something? I've never once hurt you."

Working up her nerve she rattled it off, "Do you know if my mom had another child? A daughter perhaps?" Teddy's face noticeably paled; it looked as if the color drained from his face and he staggered backwards.

Robert grabbed him and ushered him to a seat. "That was a lifetime ago, but I guess if you're asking then there is a cause for it. She did have a child, and it was a girl. She was taken when she was a baby. Your mother didn't know if she was alive or dead. She hadn't heard anything about her, that didn't keep her from looking though. I think she finally gave up because she thought God was correcting a mistake."

"What do you mean she was taken? What mistake"?
Mary B asked quickly.

"She was taken from your mother at the hospital. Are
you sure you want to hear all of this?" Mary nodded her
head. She didn't trust herself to speak.

"The mistake was she had the baby out of wedlock, and
it was the result of..." He hesitated because he hadn't
thought about this since he was first brought to the nursing
home. He had spent quite a bit of time with a therapist. This
was the part of his therapy he hadn't completed. He was
never able to tell Mary's mom, that he was sorry.

This time it was William who asked the question. "The
result of what exactly, if you don't mind me asking?"

"I raped my sister. I was sick, and I didn't want to admit
it back then. Only since I've been in this place, have I even
acknowledged it."

William's face turned to stone. Mary couldn't help
herself; she slapped the pure mess out of her uncle. "What
kind of devil are you? Who would do that to their own sister?
You shall rot in the bowels of the deepest levels of hell for
what you have done." The words erupted from her before
she could even think. Mary B didn't think he deserved to
know if he had a daughter, or possible granddaughter out
there in the world. She vowed he would die alone.

"You came here for answers, please remember that. I
asked if you really wanted to hear this. I am so sorry; I never
got a chance to tell your mom that, so I tell you now.
Whether you accept it or not, I am truly sorry." Her uncle
said, staring at the floor morosely.

Jean and Robert were already by the door; they couldn't
believe what they had just heard. They were glad that she

got the answers she needed but not the actual answers. William stood up and reached for Mary's hand, she reached out and took his hand, he pulled her to her feet and simply said, "Let's go baby, I think we're done here." Mary B didn't argue, she was thankful for the escape.

The ride home was awkward to say the least. There was so much to say, but no one was willing to say it. Robert kept thinking and praying to himself, "Please Lord, I don't know what's wrong with some of the men in our family, but I pray I don't turn out like them."

It was as if Mary B heard his prayer. "Robert, you are nothing like them. You have more of your dad in you than you think. He is a wonderful man, and never doubt that you are too. I know you and your sister have both been through some things, things most people could never imagine. I am so proud of you two, and I can never say it enough. I love you."

William chimed in, "I love you both so much. I know I don't always say it, but I hope that I do show it to you and your children." He held Mary B close to his side. It was times like these he wished he could take all her hurt and pain and make it go away. On the inside he was still mentally kicking himself because he should have left well enough alone.

Mary B asked, "What about Janet, should we even say anything? I don't know if I'd want to know my biological dad was a rapist, but then again, maybe she needs to know. Everyone can use some closure in their lives." They agreed that they would feel her out and see what she knew, or if she knew where she came from or cared to learn about her heritage.

Jean's mind was going one hundred miles per hour. It felt like her family was long overdue for some sunshine. The storm cloud had been hovering over the top of them for years. Glancing down at her phone, she realized Tim had tried calling her several times; he left four voicemails and six texts. All she could do was smile to herself, she already knew he was fussing, because she didn't call when she got there, nor did she call at any point during the visit or the return trip.

As Robert pulled into the driveway, she saw Tim walking out to meet the car. He helped her get out of the car, and into the house they went. He was being really overprotective of her since she was pregnant this time around. Tim whispered in her ear, "I want to know what happened? Is everyone okay?" Once she was safely ensconced in the house, he went out to help Mary B come in and get settled. Tim looked at William for some indication on how the trip went, but his face was unreadable. He knew it wasn't good because no one was talking. None of the joking around that they usually do, and he could see that Mary B had been crying. That wasn't something he was used to seeing. Mary B was the strongest woman he had ever met. Even when things seemed at their darkest, she found the light. She was a beacon of strength and the safety net when the world around them was full of storms. Their world had seen its fair share of storms here lately. He could tell whatever had transpired had also bothered the rest of the group.

Tim didn't want to press so he told the ladies he would run to the store and pick up some lunch. He asked if Robert wanted to ride with him.

"Yeah, sure bro, I could use a break from this right now."

"Robert man, I've never seen this family this shaken to the core. I'm not even sure that I want to know what happened today but is everybody okay. I mean like, really okay?"

Robert couldn't even lie to him, "Truthfully man, I don't know. This was a blow that I don't think my mom ever saw coming. Better yet I know she didn't see it. None of us would have thought such a thing." Robert proceeded to tell Tim the story as he was told. Tim shook his head, like there was no way.

After Robert finished talking, Tim asked, "So what's next? Are they planning on talking to Janet?"

"We were going to take the subtle approach and try to feel her out. See what all she knows, if she knows anything. Maybe she doesn't even want to know,"

"Yeah I don't imagine that it would be easy learning things about yourself that you didn't know and rather unpleasant things at that." Tim sighed a little louder than he would have liked.

"So, what can I do to help with all of this? I hate seeing them in this state, and I know they have gotten through other stuff, but I don't know how much more they can take." Robert agreed, he told Tim that they would figure it out.

By the time the guys returned from the store Robert was already planning his next move. Janet was scheduled to come by this afternoon, so he was going to make a point to be at home. He usually stayed at work or out of the house to give Davina her space so that she could be herself, and not have to worry about impressing him. Robert knew if he was in the house, she would push herself and possibly overdo it.

She had been happy with filling him in each day after her and Janet's sessions. He genuinely loved hearing about her progress, they were growing closer, and their bond was stronger than it had ever been. The children were thriving, and their family was in a good place. Robert said his good-byes to the family before he headed home.

He arrived home just as Janet was pulling up, so he thought what better opportunity to strike up a conversation. "Hey Janet, I got a question for you." With a semi puzzled look on her face she responded, "Hey Robert, sure what's going on?"

"Not too much, I just know I'm not usually around when you are here. How are things coming with Davina? Is she almost ready for dancing lessons yet?"

"Dancing lessons, not quite, but she has made some solid progress. I'm not sure that she wants me to tell you every-thing. You will have to get clearance from her, before I can tell you anything more."

"Oh, okay I see. I will ask for that clearance," he smiled, "And she will give it to me. Janet, we went to the same school, right? Did we have classes together?"

Janet was intrigued by this newfound interest that Robert had in her. She thought he was starting to come around and flirting with her. She had kept her promise to not pursue him in any way. She was being respectful of her friend Davina. Janet had come to value their friendship more and more. Yet his questions still intrigued her.

"Yeah, we were at the same school, and had some of the same classes. I used to have the biggest crush on you back then. There was just something about you and your eyes. You don't remember this apparently, but there was this one time you helped me out. It was simple enough; this guy bumped into me and made me drop my books. My papers started flying all over the place and you helped me to catch all of them. I was especially thankful, because one was a paper that I had worked really hard on, and I needed a good grade in order to pass the class. I remember telling you I owed you for life for that. After that you always smiled at me, and always spoke to me. I was a pretty lonely child growing up, so that small thing meant more than you could ever know."

Robert was at a loss for words, he didn't know that he had an impact on her. He did always feel like he was the man in school, but he knew that it was all in his mind. Robert was just your average charming guy, who tried to look out for the little guy. "Do you have family around here? Brothers or sisters?"

"You do know you're running into my session with your wife. Not that I mind catching up, but I don't want to keep her waiting."

Davina was at the door waiting when they finally made it to the front door. "Hey two of my favorite people in the whole wide world, other than my children of course."

"Hey babe," Robert leans down to kiss her. "How was your day so far? Oh, and by the way I was trying to get a report of your progress from the warden here, but she wouldn't give it up without your permission. Isn't that just crazy?"

Davina shrugged her shoulders and replied, "She is only doing what I asked. I don't want you to get your hopes up until there is really something to hope for." Looking towards Janet, she asks, "Janet, can you give us a quick moment, I just haven't seen him since this morning, and I need to ask him a question?".

"Certainly, I will go get set up and I will be back in a

few, is that okay?" Davina knew she didn't have much time, so she jumped right in questioning Robert, "How did things go this morning? Are you okay?"

Slightly agitated Robert replied, "Babe, I will have to talk to you about it later. There's a lot going on, and it's not something that we can talk about quickly, I promise we will talk as soon as she leaves today. I'm going to get the children and I'll take them to go get ice cream, so you can get busy on your session. I've held it up enough," and with that he was gone.

CHAPTER FOUR

MARY B AND WILLIAM LEFT A LITTLE AFTER ROBERT. She was feeling a little weak, and William wasn't successful in getting her to eat anything all day. He didn't want it to show but he was a bit worried about her. She always thought of him as her strong untouchable man. Truth was, he was strongest with her. When they got home, he checked her sugar levels and they were off, so he gave her an injection to help correct her levels.

"Baby, you know that you need to eat something. Can I fix you some soup or something?" William asked concernedly.

"I just want to lay down for a bit, is that okay? I just want to clear my mind and try and get some rest. I feel like I've been hit with a car, or maybe a truck." She smiled when she said that, trying to lighten the mood. William walked her to the bedroom, helped her onto the bed, removed her shoes, and tucked her in. He went to go lock up the house and brought her some water and juice back.

As soon as he walked through the bedroom door she

asked, "William could you bring me some juice and water please. I'm feeling a little dehydrated." William just smiled to himself, he knew her better than anyone.

"I have it right here baby."

"You always know what I need and when I need it." William blushed, "What can I say, I love my wife. You get some rest and I will be here when you wake up. I will never leave your side, even in death, I will always be right here." Mary B hated when he talked about death. Lord only knew she wasn't ready for anything of the sort.

Jean called Bianca and apologized for not being able to really talk earlier. She told her she was going to talk to Tim that evening and they would set up a time for Lucas and Bianca to come for a visit, or they could meet somewhere for dinner. Bianca told Jean that Lucas wanted to see Kim and promised he would be okay with just seeing her.

She told Jean that Kim was her daughter, and other than being there financially to assist and when she came of age and had questions, that would be the extent of their involvement. Bianca tried to reassure Jean that Lucas didn't want to interrupt the agreement that was already made.

"I'll call you back in the next few days or so, once Tim and I talk and come up with a time." Bianca asked her how her pregnancy was going. Jean told her that she had been a bit tired and this one was taking its toll on her body. She assured her that she was doing okay though. Jean thanked Bianca for the concern.

Once she was off the phone, she knew it was time to talk

to Tim about everything that had happened that day. She went through the house to Mia and Kim's room, there she found him reading them a story. She was so happy to have him as her baby's daddy. He was good for them all, and he didn't hesitate to show it. Jean told him when he was done, there were a few things they needed to talk about. Tim said he would come find her in just a few.

True to his word, he was out in ten minutes. She told him he better not had cut their story time short. He assured her that he did no such thing. He would never jip his baby girls or boys for that matter. She knew without a doubt he was being truthful.

"What's on your mind Jean"?

"I finally heard back from Bianca today while on the ride to Shady Acres. That was Lucas that hit us. He swears it was an accident. I am so proud of Bianca because she told him the truth, he didn't like it, but she was a big girl. She didn't want to start their life off with a lie. She hadn't given him the option to say once the child was here and that he didn't want her. So, she felt she owed it to him. She was right; I can't say that I blame her. In the end he is good with the decision, he did have one condition, he wanted to meet us officially, and he would like to see Kim." Jean could see the worry bloom on Tim's face. "She promised me, it was all going to be the way we originally arranged. He just wanted to put a face to the name, and the same with us."

"As long as you're sure Jean, I'm with you 100%, that will never change."

"Did you talk to Robert about what happened when we were at Shady Acres? I figured you would ask him." Tim had shaken his head yes.

"As you can imagine we all are disgusted. I'm more concerned about Momma than anything else. I couldn't imagine growing up without Robert, or not knowing that I even had a Robert. Mom said someone had slipped up and mentioned a sister when she was a child, but it was quickly swept back into that wretched closet, only to come out after so many years."

"Mary B was out of it today, and that was the first time I had seen her like that,"

"She was and still is, the strong one of the family. I don't know how to make it better for her, so I'm going to do what she always taught us to do and that is pray for understanding. The sad thing is that this will change lives from this day forward." The only thing Tim knew to do at that moment was to hold his wife, so she knew that she was not alone.

OVER THE NEXT FEW DAYS JANET REALIZED THAT SHE was seeing her client's family a lot more often. While she didn't mind it, they seemed awfully chatty. Usually they just left them alone to do their rehab, so it was a noticeable change. By the second week of this, she decided to ask Davina what was going on. The thing was Davina hadn't been clued in on the developments from the last few weeks, and it was for this very reason. This was done so that in the event she was asked she actually didn't know anything. Robert didn't like not sharing things with his wife, but he wanted to make sure she stayed focused on her rehab.

"Davina, hey is something going on with your family? They are hanging around you more these days. Did I do something to make them feel as if I were going to hurt you or overwork you?"

"Truly Janet, I don't know why they are acting a bit peculiar, I've noticed it myself. But I promise I don't have any idea as to what is going on. I've certainly not told them about the fact that you bully me or boss me around for hours and won't let me rest or even eat." Davina says with a wink as she laughs out loud.

Janet laughs so hard, her face turns bright red. "Well, it's only going to get worse now. I'll find out what's going on sooner or later. I've already told Robert that I wasn't going to tell him about your progress, so maybe he asked everyone else to try and get it out of me. He just doesn't know it's not going to work. I'm built tough. Sealed like a lock on Fort Knox."

DAVINA KNEW SHE WAS JOKING ABOUT IT GETTING worse. She was truly thankful for Janet's patience with her and didn't want anything to make her feel uncomfortable. She made up in her mind that she would talk to Robert that evening. Davina didn't want anything to compromise her progress. As luck would have it, she didn't have to wait to talk to Robert.

MARY B HAD BEEN TRYING TO WRAP HER MIND AROUND the earth-shattering information she now possessed. After carefully weighing out the odds, she figured the only way to proceed was to take the bull by its horns. She would just have an open and honest conversation with Janet, and she was determined to do it today. She didn't want to go through any more days of not knowing.

Mary B told William she was going to be going over to Robert's. She told him that she wanted to go ahead and talk to Janet. He asked her if she was sure about this, and she said it was something that she had to do. And just like that, he understood.

"Do you want me to go with you? I know you can handle anything that comes your way."

"Of course, I want you by my side always."

"There is no place, and I mean no place that I would rather be. What time do you want to leave?" he asked her as she came back into the room with her coat on. He could only smile to himself; he should have known. He knew who he was dealing with.

By the time they arrived at Robert's, Davina's session was just about over. William went and played with the twins, while Mary B went into the kitchen to fix them some lunch, since Davina told her that they hadn't eaten yet. She hadn't been over since they returned from Shady Acres, she wasn't sure if she was ready to face the reality. Her absence had been missed by the twins. They ran and covered her with kisses and hugged her tightly. She had been missing them too. Mary hadn't been around any of the grandchildren and that was so unlike her. She meant for that to come to an end today, they didn't deserve that, just because she had stuff on her mind. Facing it head on was the only way to make it all right again.

She watched and waited until their session was winding down, before she started in working on Janet. She knew she wouldn't be able to strike an inconspicuous conversation with her because they didn't really have anything in common that is except Davina. She figured her best approach would be to just be honest. If only someone had been honest with Mary B years ago, none of this would be happening now.

Janet was packing up some of her things that she used in her therapy sessions. Mary saw her opportunity when she was going outside with her second load. "Hey Janet, I know we don't talk a lot, but I've got something really serious to talk to you about. And unfortunately for me, I don't know any other way than to just come right out and say it."

Janet was a little taken back by Mary B's candor, but much to her surprise she appreciates it. After putting the items in the trunk of the car, she gives Mary B her full attention. "How can I help you ma'am?"

"I honestly just want to talk. I didn't mean to sound so cryptic a minute ago. Do you mind if we go and sit on the porch, I'm not as young as I used to be?" Mary B asked with a chuckle.

"Of course, I have some time before my next appointment. What would you like to discuss?"

"First of all, do you have family here?"

All kinds of thoughts ran through her mind since Mary said she wanted to talk to her. Could she have possibly picked up on the fact that she was still crushing on Robert? She couldn't possibly have known, Janet felt like she had kept it under control.

She tried keeping their conversations short and to a minimum. "That's kind of personal isn't it ma'am? I don't mean to be rude or anything, but why is that any of your business?"

"To put it simply, I think you may be my sister's child."

That wasn't the response that Janet was expecting, and she nearly fell off the porch, as Mary B said it.

"That's crazy. My mom never mentioned having a sister, or any family for that matter. She always said that she was bounced back and forth from foster home to foster home. Her adoptive parents were killed in a plane crash, when she was twelve. It was just she and I. Well, that is up until she died last year of a heart attack. How could you possibly think we are related? For years we lived around here, and I even went to school with Robert and Jean, and no one ever said anything. That would have been the perfect time, I would think while my mom was still alive." Confusion overtook Janet's face. She was questioning some things in her mind.

Mary B felt the young lady's pain. She had felt the same pain a few weeks ago. There was no easy way to soften the blow. "You are correct, it would have been better to have this conversation with your mother, but I only just recently found out these things myself. The fact that there is a strong possibility that you are related to me is one of them. There is a real simple solution that would prove that fact or disprove it. If it proves to be true, then I will tell you the rest of what I know, that is if you want to know. If it proves to be incorrect, along with my sincerest apology for bringing this up, I will never mention it again, and I hope that none of this affects your working relationship with Davina. Oh, my goodness, Robert may be seriously furious with me, because I did not consider Davina's feelings if you decided not to continue working with her. I never thought of that. I never thought out this conversation, I just knew I couldn't keep it any longer."

Janet was overwhelmed by what Mary was even eluding to. She and Davina had been making such great progress and she wouldn't let this jeopardize that. Besides she liked Davina, that was one of the reasons she hadn't made any advances toward Robert, now she was glad she didn't'. That would have been just plain out nasty, and she would never have been able to forgive herself.

"There is so much going through my mind right now, I'm not sure why this is even a conversation. But I do want to know the story of my origins if it proves to be true, and how did this all come about? Is this what has been going on for the last week or so? I've seen more of Davina's family over the past few days. I thought it was something that I had done. Even Robert has been around a lot more lately. So does the whole family know of this?"

"Pretty much everyone except for Davina, but that was simply so she wouldn't get frustrated and fall back on her progress. She has done really well from what she does tell us. I really wish there was a delicate way to handle this or discuss it, but honesty has always been my policy. And I am so sorry to have to just throw it on you like this. If you consent to a DNA test, we could have the results within a few days tops." Mary B tried her best to sound reassuring.

"That seems easy enough, what do you need from me?"

"I just need you to give a sample of your hair. Nothing painful, I promise. To make sure nothing gets contaminated, when you're ready we can go together and give our samples if you want."

"WELL IT SEEMS AS IF YOU ARE PRETTY CERTAIN OF THE results, so I have some time tomorrow before my session with

Davina, we can meet at the hospital around 9 a.m. Does that time sound okay with you?"

"Yes of course it is. My daughter Jean will also be there to give a sample, that way the results should be definitive either way. Thank you for saying you will do this. I'm sure it isn't easy for someone to disrupt your entire world."

"No, it isn't easy," Looking down at her watch she realized that time had slipped away from her, "I'm sorry but I do have to go, I'm running a bit late for my next appointment. I will see you in the morning though."

"Thank you Janet and I apologize for making you late." Janet was already to her car and waving good-bye. "Please tell Davina I said I will see her tomorrow."

As Janet was pulling out of the driveway, Robert was pulling in, and William was coming out of the house. Robert noticed that Janet didn't wave to him like normal, and she seemed rushed. Looking at his mother's face, he knew the reason. She had opened Pandora's Box and let out all its evil secrets.

"Hey Mom, please tell me you didn't tell her?" She simply nodded her head.

"Does Davina know?" Mary B shook her head again to answer.

"We talked out here as she was bringing her bags out. But I do think we owe Davina an explanation, Janet left without telling her goodbye. I think it's time that Davina knows. Janet promised me, no matter what the outcome of the test was, that she would still remain her therapist."

WILLIAM, WHO HAD BEEN SILENT SINCE HE CAME OUT

onto the porch, helped his wife up from her chair. "Are you okay?"

"Yes, I am William; I just needed to get it out, and to the one who it truly affects. I am sorry Robert that I didn't wait for you to tell Davina first. I hope you can forgive an old woman." Mary B reached out to embrace her son.

"Yeah Mom, let's go talk to Davina, I should have told her when we first got back, I hope she forgives me."

As they walked through the door Davina said she thought she heard him pull up. "Hey babe, how was your session?" Robert said, as he leaned down and pressed a kiss to his wife's forehead.

"It was good, I'm making progress. I think in the end you will be impressed and proud of how far I've come."

"I'm always proud of you my sweet. You impressed me when you came back home, and I'm in constant awe of your desire to push yourself."

"Robert love, what is going on? I can sense when you're trying to butter me up, you should know this by now. So why don't you just come clean with it. You and the rest of the family have been acting extra lately. Are you ready to tell me what happened when you all went on your little trip?" Davina asked with an arched eyebrow.

"No, I'm not ready, but I don't have a choice. I wanted to keep you out of it as long as I could, but now that is no longer possible. I will try and make this as short and sweet and uncomplicated as I can. It all started because my daddy is nosy and couldn't let something go." Robert looked pointedly at William with a side eye glance. "He thought there was a possible chance that Janet was his daughter, and the not knowing was eating away at him. He decided to do a DNA test with a few strands of my hair and a few that he got from her jacket."

Davina was in utter disbelief at this story. Her family had really lost their minds. "Anyway, the test came back that he wasn't the father but that she and I were related maternally. That means that Janet's mom would be my mom's sister. Only problem was no one knew that. So, Mom went for answers and unfortunately the ones she got were not the ones neither she nor we wanted. To make matters worse, she was conceived through rape, perpetrated by my Uncle Teddy. He assaulted his own sister and got her pregnant. The baby was stolen from the hospital. And that was the last he knew."

Mary B was the next to speak, "Davina, I talked to Janet about the possibility of her being related to me, through a sister. That probably tore her world apart, because she never knew that she had family outside of her mom. She has been put through a series of foster homes. That is no way for someone to live if they have family. We cannot change the past, but we can try and fix the future. Hopefully she will want to be a part of our family. Tomorrow she and I will be going to the hospital to take a DNA test; I told her I was going to bring Jean along so that the results would be definitive. She promised me that she would remain your therapist regardless of the results."

Davina couldn't believe what she was hearing. It all sounded like a soap opera, but only this was real, and it was her family. She wanted to reach out to Janet, but she said she would wait it out and see if she brought it up during their session tomorrow. She didn't want to stir the pot too soon. This wasn't even directly affecting Davina, but she was barely handling the influx of information. She could only imagine what Janet was dealing with. She swore to herself to be there for her no matter what.

"I hope that things work out and if she is related that's great, but if not, please for me don't treat her any different. I can only imagine if I was a horse and you dangled an apple in front of my face and then jerked it back without warning, that would hurt me just as bad." They all agreed, they hadn't thought of it that way. This was just another reason why Robert loved his wife. She made sense of his crazy world.

At that moment Jean called Robert and said that she was on her way to the hospital, she was having very severe labor pains. Robert asked was Tim with her, she said yes. He told her that he was on the way to the hospital, and that he would see her soon.

TIM WAS A BIT ON THE NERVOUS SIDE; JEAN WASN'T DUE to have the baby for another few months or so. Then there was the stress she had been under with Kim, and Bianca and Lucas, not to mention her mom, and all the craziness with Janet. He tried to stay strong for his wife, but inside he was beyond worried. Tim knew that Jean was trying to be tough, but he could see what was truly in her eyes.

Although Jean had managed to hold out this long carrying their little girl, she knew she couldn't hold onto her for the full nine months. Her doctor had warned her against anything strenuous or stressful. She had encouraged her to put her feet up as often as possible. Tim tried to ensure that advice was followed to the T, but his wife was stubborn, she would always do what she wanted, when she wanted, and how she wanted.

That night Jean was dealing with the twins, and feeding Kim, when she noticed the blood draining down her leg. Mia noticed it first, and asked her "Mom is that catsup?" That was as close to pronouncing ketchup as she could get. Jean's first response was to smile, and then she told Mia to go get her daddy, who was outside in the garage.

Tim entered the room like a whirlwind. Mia told him there was catsup where Mommy was sitting. He saw the fearful look on her face, and he removed all the children out of the room first. Then he helped his wife to the bathroom, so they could get her cleaned up, while doing that he was on the phone with the doctor. "How quickly can you get her to the hospital? Do I need to call an ambulance for her?"

"No that's not necessary, I will get her there. I just have to get my other kids situated first." Jean told him to call her mom.

He promptly tried calling the house phone, but there was no answer. As he shook his head and said no answer, Jean doubled over. She screamed out in pain but tried to muffle it so the children wouldn't be alarmed. Miles heard his mom and came to find out what was going on. He was indeed his mom's son, the more Tim told him to go stay with the others, the more he told Tim he wasn't leaving his mom. Tim couldn't even argue with him. He was proud of his son at that moment.

Miles grabbed the phone from Tim and dialed his Uncle Robert's number, when he answered he handed the phone to his mom. Jean told Robert that she was going to the hospital. Mary B and William were already out the door, and on their way to Jean's. Mary B needed to see for herself that her daughter was okay. Jean hadn't told Robert about the blood; she didn't want him to worry while they were on the way over. Tim had helped Jean to get cleaned up and he had her in the car with Miles's help by the time Mary B and William arrived.

Miles insisted that he go with her to the hospital. Jean didn't have the strength to fight him, so she agreed. "You have to behave, and whatever Tim tells you to do, you have to do it okay?"

"Yes Momma," Miles had been just as protective as Tim during this pregnancy. Things were a bit rough initially to get Miles to open up when she first came back home. She and he were still building on their bond. On the ride to the hospital he was sitting behind his mom and he was holding her hand. He was praying at the same time, Jean's heart melted. She often worried if she had damaged him, by her leaving him with Mary B.

Each time she moaned in pain, he squeezed her hand, and continued praying. Jean was trying not to show the pain, but between the cramping and the contractions she couldn't take it. The ride to the hospital seemed like it was taking forever. Just as she felt another contraction coming, Tim turned into the entrance to the hospital. Jean's doctor was waiting for them. She had a wheelchair waiting and they rushed her into the hospital and up to labor and delivery. Even if they somehow managed to prevent delivery tonight, she wouldn't be going home until after she gave birth.

CHAPTER FIVE

WHILE THEY TOOK JEAN UPSTAIRS, TIM WENT TO PARK the car. He noticed that there was a significant amount of blood in the seat. He had thought to put a towel under her just in case. Truth was he wasn't prepared for the amount he saw. When the nurses lifted his wife out of the car, she looked so weak. He knew during the car ride she was trying to be that strong woman he had married and fought so hard for. His mind went back to when he saw her sitting in the chair bleeding, and completely calm. *That was so like her,* he thought. A smile crossed his face, but it was short lived. His phone vibrates, and it's her doctor. Tim felt his heart stop, and then slowly it began beating again. The doctor needed his consent to give her some blood. She had passed out from the amount she had lost on the ride over and was still bleeding because they didn't know why just yet.

Tim said, "Yes of course, I will get Robert to come immediately. He is her twin so I know their blood will match."

"Tim you don't understand, there isn't any time to spare. She has lost too much blood. Jean and the baby are both in jeopardy right now. What about the little one that came with you?" Tim quickly told the doctor that his blood was not a match. When Jean was pregnant with Miles, she was RH negative, Miles was RH positive. Her body began to make antibodies to fight off his blood. This caused extra stress and trauma to a young Jean. Not many knew that whole truth. This mother and child would never be able to donate to each other. After Tim explained this to the Dr. he understood.

"We can give her some from the supply here; I just need your consent. The blood has been tested several times. Time is not on our side; can we proceed with treatment?" Tim told her that he could have her brother there in less than ten minutes. He knew she had to agree because either way it was going to take two hours for them to cross match it to hers. Tim had heard so many horror stories of tainted blood, and his wife's life was hanging in the balance just that quickly. He didn't even have time to think. He prayed he was making the right decision. She would never forgive him if something went wrong. He knew he would never forgive himself either.

He hung up the phone and dialed Robert's number, but quickly hung it up as he saw Robert pulling into the parking lot. By the time they got upstairs to Jean's room, the doctor had stopped the bleeding, but they were going to have to take the baby. There wasn't any time to waste; they were prepping her for the C-section. They rushed Robert to get him set up for the transfusion. Since it was her twin, they skipped a few of the protocols. The doctor had verified his blood type from Robert's chart there at the hospital; she didn't want to lose her license for blatantly disregarding the rules.

The doctor came out to speak to Tim; she wanted to explain what was happening and why things were moving so fast. "Listen, the situation with your wife is indeed serious; she has what is called a uterine rupture. This means her muscles are too weak, probably from her last pregnancy. Because of this the baby has moved into her abdomen. This is very dangerous as you can imagine." Tim was a nurse, but this part was outside of his purview.

His nerves were all over the place; he remained silent while the doctor talked. "We are going to be doing two things at once with her, we are actually going to take Robert's blood and infuse it directly into her bloodstream while in the operating room, because she is too weak to do anything else. If we are to make a valiant effort to save her and the baby, this is what has to happen. It's called a direct blood transfusion. I will tell you as much as I can while we are going through the process. I will let you be on the other side of the curtain with Robert while we are working on Jean. We are going to do everything in our power to bring both of these ladies out of this healthy."

Tim was afraid to use his words, so he simply shook his head. He trusted this doctor; his father went to med school with her. Tim thanked her and said, "Do whatever has to be done to save them both." It took a bit to get her vitals stable enough to do the C-section, they were concerned about her crashing during surgery, but she did well.

During the next few hours a baby was brought into the world, she was fighting all the way. Jean was stable but still extremely weak; she was out cold during the delivery, and the stitching up phase. It was for the best; in her state she wouldn't have been much help. They did a tubal ligation; bringing any more children into the world would literally kill Jean.

Normally those decisions were made with the mother's consent, but there was no time, the doctor had mentioned it to Tim, and he agreed. Jean and he had already discussed not having any more children and this just made it official. It was just one less thing to worry about later. Jean's color was starting to come back. Robert unfortunately had to remain hooked up to Jean for another hour, they didn't want the blood fusing too quickly, nor did they want him to give too much.

After the surgery, they put Jean into a recovery room. When she came to, she was in the room with Robert. She began trying to piece everything that had happened together. She remembered that she was at home and the contractions began, there was a lot of blood, and from there it was fuzzy. She clearly didn't have a baby in her tummy anymore that much she could tell. Jean knew she was in the hospital of course, she didn't know why Robert was there, unless she had lost that much blood, and they used him for a transfusion.

She couldn't stop her mind from running all over the place. Where was Tim? What happened to the baby? Why is Robert asleep and slobbering? She would have to pick at him later about that. Jean smiled at that thought. She also laughed because she knew she was a little loopy from the medication they must have given her.

Thankfully Tim walked in and smiled at her, when he saw she was awake. "Woman, you know how to scare the mess out of me don't you? How are you feeling?" Jean scratched her head and mumbled something. Again, she smiled to herself, because when she was asking all those questions in her head, she sounded just fine, but when she tried to speak it was muffled.

Tim being a nurse began checking to see what medications she was still getting through the IV. Her nurse had kept the pain medicine dripping at the quicker rate. He changed it to drip slowly, he was eager for her to come around completely. He needed to make sure that she was okay. Tim was thankful that she had her color back and had woken up, but he needed her to have a conversation with him. He wanted to make sure she knew what had occurred. He didn't want any secrets, or for her not to know everything that had to be done.

Just then the nurse brought the baby in. Tim hadn't seen the baby until now, and he had to say she was the most beautiful baby he had ever seen. In his eyes, she was absolutely perfect. Not to say his twins weren't perfect also, or Miles, Dayshaun, or even Kim. There was something about this little girl. In that moment he knew she would be someone special, and he would give her the world, she had already stolen his heart.

Jean looked at her daughter and the only word she was able to utter was "Raven," and so it was, the newest addition to their family had a name. Jean smiled and dozed off to sleep just like that. Tim held his daughter as if he was holding his first child ever. She opened her eyes and she had those stormy gray eyes. Tim could only smile to himself. He knew those eyes had been the cause of a lot of drama within their family. His daughter was going to be the opposite.

After feeding her, he took her back to the nursery, taking care to make sure she was identified correctly. Tim went to go and get Miles from the waiting room, he had been checking on him every so often, and the aides were also. Miles went to the nursery to see his new sister, he told Tim that he approved. He said she was pretty. After being there for a few minutes he asked if he could see his momma. Tim told him that she might be sleeping, he said he didn't care he just wanted to see her, to make sure she was okay.

When they entered the room, she was asleep, but it was like she felt him enter the room. She turned her head and looked at him, saying his name before she even saw him. Miles went to her and he grabbed her hand, and he prayed again for her. Jean didn't know what to say, but she was thankful that her son knew the power of prayer. When he finished, he kissed her cheek, and told her to rest, that he would be back tomorrow, and he said he knew she was tired.

Tim just watched in amusement; Miles was older than his eight years. He was too smart and articulate for his own good, this made Tim proud and honored to be his father.

When Janet came the next day for their therapy session Davina noticed that she was more reserved then when they first started. Her heart went out to Janet; she of all people knew what keeping secrets could do to a family. She tried to give Janet her space, but midway into their session, Davina just stopped. Janet was confused; she didn't know what was happening.

"Okay Janet that's it, I'm done for the day. I am no longer feeling motivated to keep pushing forward. Maybe I will just give up and stay where I am. What do you think about that Janet?"

Janet was still confused as she replied, "What is going on? Why would you give up on what you have done? You have come so far and made great strides."

To this Davina simply smiled. "Yep, so why would you give up on our friendship? We've worked so hard and come so far; you've kept me motivated. Even when I wanted to give up on myself, you kept on pushing. So how do I look allowing you to give up on this? I understand you don't have to talk about the events that have recently occurred, but for you to not talk to me at all and treat me like a stranger is not okay."

Janet could only half smile at her, Davina just didn't understand. It wasn't easy; this new knowledge was messing with her mind. Janet knew she didn't know all the details yet, but just the fact that she potentially has family. She had been alone for a while now. What if she couldn't handle being a part of one? She was thankful for Davina and her friendship, it meant more than she would ever be able to express to her friend. At the time when she needed someone the most, and something to keep her focused, there came this case. No one knew what skeletons she had in her closet.

She was no good with relationships; Janet managed to finally escape an abusive relationship. After two years, not all bad, she had escaped from Bo, her own private nightmare. Her ex-boyfriend had come close to killing her on more than one occasion. The last time was the worse. The accident that she was in, that pinned her between two cars, was no accident at all.

Bo had been so nice and kind when they first met. He promised her the world, and in the beginning, he gave it to her. Then slowly things started changing. She noticed he would take off work, to be at home when she was off. That wasn't much to be concerned about, but then when she was working, he would show up to her client's homes unexpectedly. Bo always had an excuse though, and he could charm his way through anything. He would say he locked his keys in the house, or that he left his phone so he couldn't call ahead. The worst one was when he said he just had to see her.

At first, she just thought he was overprotective, and that he genuinely missed her. She didn't want to believe he was out of his mind. Janet had always been alone, especially when her stepdad took her brother and went back to his homeland of Africa. She was tired of being alone. When Bo showed interest and began pursuing her, she thought it was cute. No one had ever shown her this much attention before. Bo had joked around; at least she thought he was joking, that if he couldn't have her, then no one else would. He would use that line when they were out and about, and a guy stared for more than two seconds. This happened fairly often, Janet was an attractive lady, but that was usually as far as it went.

There was this one-day that Janet was talking to a coworker as they were leaving work. It just so happened to have been a male coworker named Joe. He was talking to Janet about his girl breaking up with him, and how it had really torn him up. They had been talking for about fifteen minutes or so, when her phone rang. Silly her, she didn't even look at it; she thought that would be rude, especially since her friend was going through something. About five minutes later it rang again, and again she didn't answer. Within five more minutes, her phone vibrated, it did that when she received a text message. She finally looked at her phone, and it was Bo. The text simply read, "Bang, Bang, he's dead."

Just then she saw Bo's car pull up and he rolled his window down. Janet couldn't believe the fact that he had his gun pointed at Joe. Thankfully Joe's back was turned so he couldn't see what he was doing; embarrassed at Bo's intrusion she cut the conversation short and told Joe she had to go. She hurried to her car and got in and drove home. Bo beat her there and was furious when she arrived.

She wasn't even out of the car good when he started yelling at her. "Yo Janet, that's what you do? You going to disregard me for that dude? I know you seen me calling you. You didn't even think to answer your text message."

"I'm sorry Bo, Joe just needed to talk. His girlfriend broke up with him. That's all that was going on I promise." Janet cried tearfully.

"I don't care about that fool. I was trying to ask you what you wanted for dinner and you ignored me for him."

"I said I'm sorry Bo. I didn't mean to; I would never ignore you. I love yo...." that was all she could get out before he punched her in the face.

He had his hands around her neck so fast she couldn't move even if she tried. He gripped her tightly until she was on the brink of passing out. In the last possible second, he released her, and she dropped to the floor. Her color was gone from her face, she couldn't focus, and she knew he was going to kill her.

She laid there until he walked away from her, but not before kicking her. "You will respect me. No woman of mine will be talking to some dude. You will learn not to disrespect me. I already told you, if I can't have you no one will."

Janet stayed on the floor for an hour until he came and picked her up and carried her to the bed. He told her, he was sorry, he said he just gets jealous sometimes. He promised her that he didn't mean it. "I just love you so much Janet, I don't want to lose you, I can't lose you." Tears drained from her eyes from the pain, when he kicked her, he had broken a rib. With no other relationship to compare hers to, Janet thought this was love. She shouldn't have ignored his call; it was her fault. It had to be, why else would he have done that. He had never acted like that before. Janet didn't realize that was just the beginning.

She stayed with him for years after that, she thought she had nowhere to go, and she was scared for her life. There were more times like that as well as the final blow. When he pinned her between the cars, she knew if she lived, she had to leave. Thankfully they made her stay in the hospital and then they transferred her to a specialty rehab center. No one, except her doctor knew where she had gone.

For two years she was unable to walk, but she kept pushing herself and finally she was able to walk again. At first, she needed a walker, then eventually she was able to use a cane and then finally she had done it unassisted. She moved away from there and never looked back, now a few years later she finds out that she is no longer alone in this world. If only she had someone back then, maybe her nightmare would not have happened.

She realized she had jumped back in time. Davina was looking at her and calling her name "Janet, Janet, are you okay? Where did you go?"

Janet assured her she was okay, just thinking back on her past she told her. "Davina, I know you're just trying to help me, and I do appreciate it. I will be okay and back to normal soon. I promise. I do value our friendship. It's just a lot to try and cope with all at once." Janet felt it best to try and change the subject, "So are you finished for today, or are you feeling motivated? If you're done its fine, I'm kind of tired myself, but if not let's get busy." Davina told her to go ahead and they would pick back up tomorrow.

CHAPTER SIX

A FEW DAYS LATER, MARY B RECEIVED A CALL FROM THE lab; they said the results of the DNA test were in. The lab tech asked if she wanted to come in and get the results, or did she want the individuals to get their own. She knew some people were funny about that. Mary told them to give her a day to contact everyone involved and see what they wanted to do. Although Mary B was expecting the results, she wasn't completely prepared for them, and now there was the birth of Raven. There was a lot going on right now. Well Jean was already at the hospital, so that was one less person to call. She was actually not too enthused about calling Janet. Mary knew what it felt like to hear something you couldn't even imagine. And up until a few days ago, this woman thought she was alone with no family and now she was potentially going to be added to this dysfunctional group. They weren't all bad of course.

Mary called over to Davina's, she knew it was her therapy time. She was almost certain that Janet was there. When Davina answered, she asked if she could speak to

Janet, "Of course, let me check to make sure she has time to talk."

Janet took the phone from Davina, "Ummm hello, yes ma'am I'm ready to get the results. What do you need me to do? Okay I will be there in about an hour. Is that okay? I will see you then."

After hanging up the phone, Janet filled Davina in on the conversation she just had with Mary B. "I would say wish me luck, but I don't think that is appropriate somehow." They both laughed, that was the first genuine laugh they had shared since the DNA thing came up. *It felt good to laugh again,* Janet thought to herself.

The hard part was over, Mary thought to herself. She was glad that Janet didn't seem upset about the results or like she didn't want to know. That would make whatever the results were easier to take in. Robert was still at work, so she left him a voicemail to meet her in Jean's room at the hospital as soon as he got off.

"Well William, you ready to see the results of what you started?" Mary B couldn't resist an opportunity to blame this all on him. She kept telling him, if only he hadn't been so nosy none of this would be happening. William would just shake his head. William knew that she knew he never meant to cause any drama with this issue, but this would stick with him. He felt bad about the way it was happening, but he was quick to tell Mary B that everything happened for a reason. He knew that would shut her up, it always did.

As they prepared to head to the hospital, Mary was fumbling with her jacket, William helped her to fasten it, and he pulled her in close and hugged her. "It's going to be alright," his words comforted her at that moment. She was grateful to have him by her side, through all the good and bad they had to endure.

Mary B and William were the first to arrive at the hospital, so they went and picked up the envelopes from the lab. All envelopes were sealed, and each person's name was written across the seal. That was to show everyone that no one had looked at the results. The tech told them to page her when they were ready and she would be in the room to help interpret the results if they needed it, but she said she had written up an additional document explaining the results, which was included within each of the envelopes. Mary B thanked her, and she and William headed up to Jean's room.

Robert was just getting off the elevator as Mary B and William came around the corner. "Hey Mom and Pop, fancy meeting you two here." They smiled and hugged and entered Jean's room. She was sleeping when they first walked in, but she started stirring when she heard the door ease open. Jean looked over and was happy to see her family. It had been a moment since they were all together, and she had missed that closeness. Things had especially been tense since the trip to see Uncle Teddy. She could see the stress in her mom's eyes, and she didn't like it, but she didn't know what to do, or how to fix it. Jean knew that this was a step in the direction of recovery. Once it was proven or disproven, then the healing could begin.

Jean saw the envelopes in Mary B's hands. "Are those the results? Can I see mine?" Mary B held tightly to the envelopes, "No, you may not. You will wait just like we all have to. We will open them together. Janet should be here in a few, so exercise patience."

"But Mom, please let me just peek. Come on just a tiny

little peek." Jean knew that her mom would not give in, but she always had fun pretending she was that little innocent faced child and asking her mom for the world and getting it. At least that is how it was, back when she was still an innocent, but that seemed like more than a lifetime ago.

Finally, the wait was over, Janet had arrived. Everyone said their hellos, and then Mary went on to explain the envelopes and what was included inside. She asked if there were any questions, everyone nodded no. Mary handed William the envelopes, so that once he passed them out, he could do the opening countdown.

William asked, "Is everyone ready? I know that I'm not, but we are here now. So, let's do it shall we?" William made a production out of passing out the envelopes, which was odd because usually he tended to be a bit more reserved, but in his defense, he was trying to lighten the mood. He wasn't sure that it was working, but he was determined to try his best, he owed that to his family. He saw a few smiles, so he knew his little show wasn't too bad.

Now that Jean, Janet, and Mary B all had their envelopes, he asked Robert to do the drum roll. William didn't want his son to feel left out by not having an envelope to open. Robert did as he was instructed, and William told them all to open their envelopes and to read what it said to themselves. He didn't have to read the results for himself; he could see in each of their eyes the confirmation of what he knew all along.

Janet was the first to speak; she had tried to prepare herself for this moment. It was still a shock. "Is this for real? If I'm reading this correctly, it says that we are in fact related on the maternal side. I guess that means that this also comes with a story huh? Let's have it. I want to know; well I need to know whatever you know." Up until this point Janet had been standing, Robert saw that her legs buckled a bit, so he offered her a seat.

Accepting it, she sat down, and her hands were still shaking. When she spoke her voice was trembling, and she hated that. She really wanted to be in more control of at least herself. "Are you ready for this? You may not like it all, but you have to just listen." Janet nodded her head; she didn't trust herself to speak at that moment.

"I want to start this off by saying, and I believe everyone here will agree that we are happy that you are now a part of our family. We aren't the biggest family, but you best believe that we take care of our own. You will never have to wonder if we will be there. As long as there is breath in our bodies, you have family and you will never have to go through anything else alone. Now, that was the easy part, now for the not so easy part. The results of the test show, that your mom, was my sister. I grew up as an only child, never knowing I had a sister, so imagine my surprise. In a few days' time I learned I had a sister, and I learned that she was no longer with us. I learned of a niece I had no knowledge of, and it was by sheer coincidence at this point, due to my nosy husband." William, Mary B, and Robert all sat down at this point, because they knew the conversation was not going to be a quick one.

Janet let out a deep sigh, as Mary B continued. "What we knew first, before all the DNA testing came into play, was that my William and your mother used to date, before him and me got together. You were born awhile after they had broken up, and he helped your mom provide for you and he looked after you for your first few years. You used to go to our church, so he was able to keep an eye on you. Then she moved you away, we think possibly that was when she started seeing your stepfather." Mary B stopped and asked if she was okay and if she wanted to continue.

She assured her by shaking her head that she was okay. And Mary B took a deep breath and continued, "The story of your mom's beginning is a bit difficult to hear; at least it was for me. She was the product of a rape, which happens a lot more than we like to admit, but the difference is, that my mother was raped by her own brother. His name is Theodore or Teddy for short. We learned what we know of this from him. If you'd like to meet him, we will take you to see him; I don't think it wise to go by yourself. He told us that when my mom gave birth to your mother, someone took her from the hospital. She had looked everywhere to try and find her child and she never really stopped, but there was no luck, the police weren't much help back then. Only a few people apparently knew of her giving birth to another child, and they were told to never mention it. When I was a little girl, someone mentioned once that I had a sister, but my mother told me they didn't know what they were talking about. I took her for her word. I guess in her mind she didn't want me worrying about something we couldn't control, and the fact she didn't want to answer the other questions that would come along with the knowledge. I don't think I would have blamed her. So that is pretty much the extent of what we know. I am so sorry that you had to grow up in foster homes."

Janet had been quiet, taking everything in and she finally spoke, she thought it was as good a time as any to come clean about her crush on Robert. "I guess it's a really good thing I never told you that I had a crush on you huh?" She was looking at Robert while she said this. His eyes got super big, he really had no idea, so that would explain why he had caught her looking at him when she was over during her sessions with Davina.

"Umm yeah pretty much. Maybe we shouldn't tell Davina that part, we can just keep that between those in this room." Janet agreed with Robert, she told them that she appreciated the friendship that she and Davina were building.

"I appreciate you all filling me in on all of this. I was prepared for it in my mind, but I really wasn't in my heart. So now I have cousins, an aunt and uncle, and a grandfather, who just so happens to be a nasty ol' man. Guess I will not be adding him to the Christmas card list." She tried to say with a upbeat tone. They could feel her pain, although she was trying to make light of the situation. They truly felt for her.

Jean was the next to speak. "Each of us in this room right now, unfortunately have been through some things in our lives, but we survived. It's not things that we like to talk about too often, but if it will help you to feel like a part of the family, by us sharing that part of us, then we will. Don't worry we won't do it all today, or even at one time. Besides it is far too much for one sitting. The main thing is that we got through it together. We never have given up on each other, and we never will. Thankfully the people that married my brother and I, are just as loyal and trustworthy, as I'm sure that you see for yourself with Davina. We are here for you and I hope that you will see that in time."

Mary B got up and walked over to where she was sitting

and offered her hand. When Janet stood up Mary B hugged her, and it wasn't just a hug from a neighbor, Janet felt it to the depths of her soul. She had finally found her place. She found home. Although she had been brave up until that point, when Mary B hugged her tears fell. She couldn't hold them back any longer. Through her sniffles she managed a simple, "Thank you. Thank you for bringing me home."

Mary B just held her close and rocked her, just as she did with her own children. She thought to herself, *thank you Lord; we made it through, although we took the long way around to get here. Thank God that we made it.*

CHAPTER SEVEN

BIANCA CALLED JEAN'S PHONE BUT DIDN'T GET AN answer, so she tried Tim's, and he answered. Bianca told Tim that she and Lucas would be in town in a few days and wanted to know if it was a good time for them to meet. Tim informed her that Jean had just had the baby a few days ago and would be still in the hospital. He tried to briefly explain the events surrounding the birth of their baby girl Raven. Bianca was even more excited and was ready to come that day. Tim gave Jean the phone, he had hoped she would tell her that it wasn't a good time, but no such luck, his wife was just as excited to see Bianca. Jean wanted an opportunity for Bianca to finally see Kim.

No time like the present, plus Jean had an ulterior motive, if Lucas and Bianca decided they wanted Kim back, then now was as good as any. Jean wasn't going to give her up without a fight. She and Tim had both become very attached to the little girl, not to mention the children had already bonded with her too. "If you guys don't mind meeting Tim and I here at the hospital then you are most welcome to come. I can ask Tim to bring Kim, if you would like?"

"If you are sure, we wouldn't want to intrude. Tim told me you had quite a traumatic experience." Bianca exhaled a sigh of relief. Jean was so understanding of all of this.

"Yeah I lost a lot of blood; thank God for me having a twin, I didn't have to go through with using some unknown persons." Tim was glad that he opted for that route, versus them using someone else's; he realized more and more that his wife would not have been happy with that decision. He was so thankful that he had gotten in touch with Robert that night.

Bianca ended the phone conversation with the promise to see Jean soon, within the next few days.

The next few days went by in a blur, Jean was trying to get into a rhythm of feeding Raven and resting when she did, it was easier to say than to do. She thought that once she got home with Raven it would get easier and better. The doctor was pleased with the progress that they both had made over the last few days and was talking about letting them go home. Jean asked Tim, if he would be able to stay home with her, just for a few days to make sure things went smoothly.

Tim knew that she was still concerned and haunted about what had happened only a few years before. She didn't want to ever think that she was capable of harming her child, or any child for that matter. Since Tim had gotten back and before he left to go get Christian, he was working overtime like crazy. He was planning on being home with Jean and the baby for at least the first month. Tim hadn't shared that with Jean until this moment. Christian was also still there as well. He knew Jean's past and he was willing to help. He and

Tim had already been planning. Christian oversaw the boys, while Tim had the girls, which seemed about right because the girls were Daddy's little girls. At least that is what Jean always said.

As promised, Bianca called and said that she and Lucas had just made it to town and wondered what a good time would be to stop by a visit. "Tim, just left to go get Kim and bring her up her to the hospital, so can you give us about an hour?" Bianca told her yeah, that way she had time to stop by one of her favorite shoe stores.

Jean called Tim to make sure he was on his way back soon. "Babe, I'm coming, I had to feed her and get her washed up. She was sleeping when I got here, she was looking so peaceful, I couldn't make myself wake her up, so I laid down with her."

"So, it's a good thing I called then right?" Jean asked with a wry chuckle.

"Well yeah, baby girl and I were out."

Jean loved the relationship that Tim had with all of their children. He would always do something that would make her thankful that he chose her.

Tim made it back to the hospital a whole five minutes before Bianca walked in Jean's room. Following close behind her was Lucas. Seeing him in the light, he was quite handsome Jean noted. Looking at Kim she could see the resemblance. She would be a nice blend of the two.

Bianca introduced Tim and Jean to Lucas, and she glowed as she did so. Jean thought the way that Bianca was looking at Lucas must be the way she looked at Tim. Lucas looked at Bianca the same way. That made her heart feel good, to know that even though they didn't want to raise Kim, they were still capable of love.

Lucas spoke up, "It is a pleasure to meet you both. I know you must think we are crazy not wanting to raise our own child. I assure you that is not the case." He turned to Tim at that moment and asked if he could hold her. Tim gave her up hesitantly. "Just make sure you give her back," he joked. Jean knew Tim wasn't joking, she knew he would move heaven and earth to make sure Kim and all of the children were safe.

Jean noticed that Bianca had moved away from where Lucas was standing while he was holding the baby. She had gone to look out the window. Jean noticed that she still hadn't looked at Kim yet. "Tim, can you and Lucas go down to the nursery and get Raven so that she can meet Bianca, that will give me and miss lady here a moment to catch up."

"Sure Jeannie, Lucas my man, are you ready to set eyes on another gorgeous baby? I am abundantly blessed with all these beautiful women in my world."

Lucas smiled, "Yeah man, let me meet the other young lady of the house,"

"We will be back shortly, and I will bring baby girl with me." Tim kissed his wife and left out the door.

Jean sat up a little more in the bed. "Bianca what is it? You should know me well enough to know that I can tell when something is wrong. Why won't you look at Kim? You have yet to really see her,"

"I'm scared to; Lucas is the one who needed to see her. I don't want her face to haunt me for the rest of my life. I know why I gave her to you, and I stand by that, but a part of me can't help but wonder what if I had kept her?"

"This is what I was afraid of Bianca; I thought it would be more Lucas than you though. That is one of the reasons I need you to look at your baby girl. You have to face her, so that you can release her. You already know I told you, when she gets of age, she will know who you guys are, if that is your wish. We are never going to lie to her. That's not the type of people we are. The same way that we told my older boys that she was coming to live with us, and they knew Mommy still had a baby in her tummy. I lied so much when my life depended on it, that I promised myself if I can't get through life with the truth it isn't worth it. So, tell me what is it? What is really going on? Do you think she will somehow hate you, because you gave her up? I can't promise you that she won't question it, but she will be in a loving home, so it isn't like she will be missing anything or needing anything. There will probably come a time when she will want to know you and Lucas, and that is fine by Tim and me. We would never deny her, or you guys that option. We are okay if you want to be a part of her life now, but what we do not want is you guys just coming and going with no regards to how she will feel. You feel me? You've entrusted her to us for a reason, and I, well we, take that just as serious as if she was one of our own. I will ask you now Bianca, do you want her back? If so, now is the time to speak up, because I won't offer her back to you again. You will never know how much that just hurt my heart to do that just now. She isn't an item to give away with ease."

"Jean, I know you think I'm horrible. I promise you I'm not. It's just I've never been through this before and I thought I could handle just walking away from her. Lucas and I have talked at length, and we are really both okay with her being with you. I think Lucas likes Tim, and I know he likes you too. You are giving us an opportunity to live the life we want, the one we planned. We are forever thankful for that. I know I need to face that little girl, and that way I can stop being so hard on myself. At least it isn't like some people who give up their child and they don't know where they will end up. I'm constantly reminded that I made the right choice. Thank you, Jean, you could have told me no. And if you had, and I had to raise her, I probably would have regretted her and blamed everything bad in my life on her, and that is no way to live."

"Bianca, you are a good-hearted person, always believe that. Otherwise you would have done something crazy instead of choosing your child's parents. Then again, some people might think that the way you went about that was a little unorthodox. But it is working out." Jean looked over at the door just as Tim was walking in.

"Bianca, look at their new baby girl Raven, isn't she beautiful?" Lucas was holding Raven, and Tim was holding Kim, and Jean thought to herself, *we are so dysfunctional.* Bianca surprisingly went towards Tim and reached her arms out to hold Kim, Tim handed her over. Bianca walked over to the window and was looking out and whispering something to Kim. Jean knew it was hard for her, but she knew she had to make peace with her decision, or it was going to eat her up for the rest of her life. She was proud of her at that moment.

After a few minutes Bianca handed Kim back to Tim and she kissed her on the forehead, and she then asked Lucas for Raven. "Lucas, are you really okay with the decision that I made with giving her to Tim and Jean? If you aren't, I will understand and we can make it right, but we will only have this one chance before too much time has passed."

Lucas grabbed Bianca's hand; he pulled her close and hugged her tightly. "Baby I won't lie you look really good holding our baby girl, and even little Miss Raven here, but I am really okay with the choice that was made. I wish it was made together, but I understand the reasons why. I think you did an awesome job with the parents you picked for her. She will be loved more than enough with them." Looking at Tim and then to Jean, "That was my point in meeting you guys officially, and I really do want to apologize about the fender bender. That was purely coincidence. I just wanted to make peace and have some closure when it came to that little girl over there. She seems to love her daddy. And I know the bond you all have couldn't be closer, even if it was blood linked. I made it very clear to B, that I didn't want any children, and it does have something to do with the way I grew up, but I don't think I'm capable of loving a child the way they need to be loved or should be loved. Sure, it's easy for me to be all goo goo ga ga over them now, but that is the extent. I know one day she may want to know me or us, and I'm okay with that. Don't get me wrong, she is beautiful, and I can see me in her as well a bit of B. I know without a doubt she will be cared for more than what I can ever give her. B told me that she had an account set up to help provide for her, and her education, so we will make sure that we take care of that. I can't say it enough that I am thankful that she found you. It's not easy to give up your child, but when you can pick the parents that makes it a little easier, and it is a bonus when they are pretty awesome."

Raven started fussing, it was her feeding time. Bianca

and Lucas used that as a way to make their exit. They told Jean and Tim that they would see them soon though. After they left, Jean looked at Tim and wiped her forehead, "Whew! I thought they were going to change their minds. I kept thinking that they were going to say, they wanted her back. I actually told her that if she wanted her then they needed to do it now, thankfully she said no. My heart stopped for a moment."

Tim couldn't help but feel a little relieved also. He didn't want Jean to know that he was thinking the same thing. He had become quite attached and wouldn't have been able to bear it if they tried to take her. Tim kissed his baby girl on the forehead and promised that he would always protect her.

Jean told Tim that she was glad that they had met Lucas and had everything out in the open. "It must have been hard for Lucas, even though he said he didn't want any children. Actually, seeing them for the first time, touching them, even their smell is enough to make me fall in love a million times over. I know I left Miles when I was younger, I promise that I didn't know what I was doing, but I know that I would never be able to willingly walk away from any of them. They are my world, along with you, you all give me life." Tim knew what she meant; he never thought he would be a dad, much less to a group of wonderful children. Now they could rest a little easier and not have to wonder if Bianca or Lucas would come to claim their child.

When Lucas and Bianca left the hospital, they stopped and grabbed a late dinner. Over dinner they talked about their little girl. Lucas was the first to bring her up, "We did make a beautiful little girl didn't we B?"

"Yes, we did. And I don't regret having her and giving

her to a loving family. We do have some good genes. She has your eyes, and your chin. This was why I told Jean that I didn't want to look at her. I didn't want to look into those innocent eyes and feel like I made a mistake."

Lucas grabbed her hand and told her, that if and when the time was right, perhaps they would try parenting. He reminded her that she didn't make a mistake and that she could see her daughter anytime. Jean had promised they could be a part of Kim's life.

"Yeah, I know, they are terrific. I know Kim will be fine with them." Lucas told her to put it out of her mind. He told Bianca to focus on the life that she always dreamt of. "Wherever you want to go and whatever you want to do we will. We will travel the world." Bianca smiled; he knew what made her happy.

CHAPTER EIGHT

JANET WAS STILL GETTING USED TO THE IDEA OF HAVING a family. It was a little weird she admitted to herself. She confided in Davina a lot and was thankful for her friendship. Janet was glad that it didn't seem as if the relationship was forced otherwise, she would have taken off. She was used to being on her own and running away to keep herself safe. She was tired of running. Just then her phone rings. She didn't recognize the number, so she decided to let it go to voicemail. She would check it later, no rush.

Janet decided to go ahead and take her shower and get ready for bed. She hadn't thought any more about the phone call until after she finished her shower and was turning back the covers on her bed. Her phone rang again. Janet checked the time, it was after 12 am, and again the number was not one she recognized. Again, she thought it best to let it go to voicemail. She shrugged the phone calls off and went to bed.

As luck would have it, or maybe it was bad luck, she had a restless night. She kept having the same dream over and over again. When the morning came and it was time to wake, she was exhausted. She had tossed and turned all night. She was fighting for her life, the dream she had was about Bo, and he was trying to kill her all over again. She woke up looking for him, the dream felt so real. Instinctively she checked the doors and the windows to make sure everything was locked up tight. Her heart was racing until she checked them all. She calmed a little once they were all checked, and the house was secured. Why was she dreaming about Bo after all this time? She pushed it to the back of her mind.

Over the next few months, she dreamt the same dream a few more times. Janet would always put it out of her mind. She never thought it possible that Bo would still be looking for her. Janet knew that she needed to be able to protect herself if he did ever track her down. She purchased a Glock 9mm compact and started going to the gun range. When she wasn't with Davina she was at the range. She was getting pretty good. Janet also started taking a self-defense class. She knew she could never be too careful when it came to Bo. Unfortunately, she knew all too well what he was capable of. She knew it could be ten times worse since she last saw him. Janet would never forget the look in his eyes. It was like his soul wasn't there anymore, only an evil void was left. No matter how much she tried, she couldn't shake the feeling that he was still looking for her. Her worst fears were about to come true.

DAVINA HAD PROGRESSED A LOT OVER THE NEXT FEW months. She had regained the feeling completely in her legs. That was her motivation to keep going. Davina started walking more and more. She used a walker to help steady herself for a while. She didn't like how the walker made her feel. She wasn't a granny, and she didn't want to look like one. She would practice walking when her sessions with Janet were over each day. Pretty soon she was using only the crutches. That didn't last long; she grew tired of them as well. Davina was determined to push herself harder and harder.

On the day of her anniversary with Robert she walked without any assistance for the first time. Davina had already made reservations at Robert's favorite spot and secured a babysitter for the evening. Mary B was excited to help out. She didn't get over to see the babies as much as she had been. Besides Davina was about to make her son happy, and nothing would have kept her from being a part of this occasion. Davina asked Janet to come along and help celebrate their success. She told her she couldn't have done it without her help.

"You should spend the time with your husband. I'm sure he is just dying to get you alone anyway. He told me how you two used to go out dancing when you were younger. I'm almost certain, he would like to try those legs out. You know take them for a spin."

Davina could only laugh at her. "You have been in a funk lately, so you are coming with us. Hopefully this will help get you back to the cheerful person that I first met. I know your life has changed but it's not all bad. After all we are family. What could possibly be grander than that? Well, I guess it could have happened another way, but I'm happy to have you in my life just the same. So, you see, you have to come. Please say you will. Come on."

Reluctantly, Janet agreed. "Do I have a choice in the matter? How do you know that I didn't have plans? I could have had a date."

Davina's facial expression showed that she didn't believe her one iota, so she decided to call her bluff. "You can always bring them along as well. Uh-huh, just like I thought. So, I will see you at 8." Janet knew when she was beaten, and she agreed to meet them later.

Janet got home and showered and changed and was headed out the door to meet Davina and Robert when her phone rang. This time no number showed up, it just came up as private. She decided not to answer it and allow it to go to voicemail. She had decided that this was happening too frequently so she would go ahead and get her number changed. Janet hated change more than anything, but this seemed like the best thing to do.

When she arrived at the restaurant Davina and Robert had just arrived and were waiting for her at the bar. She waved to them, and they came to meet her so they could be seated. As she was walking to her seat, she felt someone brush up against her. She didn't make a big deal about it; besides they were moving fast. When they were seated at their table, Janet asked did anyone see the guy that had rushed past them. They both said no that they weren't paying attention; Janet couldn't blame them; they were excited about Davina being able to walk again.

Once they ordered their drinks, the ladies excused themselves and went to the restroom. When they left out of the bathroom Janet walked right into Bo. Her heart stopped. Her jaw dropped. She was frozen and could not move. Davina walked into her when she stopped suddenly. The look on

Janet's face was one of pure horror. The color had drained from her face; she was as pale as a ghost.

"Hey Janet, it has been awhile since I've seen you, but I would know you anywhere." She couldn't speak, nor move. She thought she could handle it if this day ever came, but she almost wet her pants. Had she not just used the restroom she surely would have. She knew she couldn't allow him to see that she was scared. He didn't need to know that he still had that effect on her. She thought maybe she could pass it off that she didn't remember him, but she knew he would know she was lying.

She gathered her voice, "Hi Bo, how is it going? How have you been?"

"I've been okay, I've missed you though. I'm definitely glad to see you up and about and doing well. Maybe we can catch up sometime? Let me give you my card and you can call me when you're free." Janet hesitantly reached for the card, she dared not tell him no. She didn't know what he would do, and she didn't want a scene in the middle of the crowded restaurant. As she was walking away with Davina on her heels, he calls out "I'll see you soon,"

Janet barely made it to the table before her knees went weak. She tried to act like everything was normal, but Bo still scared her. When they got back to the table, Robert asked what was wrong; he could see Janet was rattled. Davina told him that she saw her ex by the bathroom. Robert knew some of what Bo had put her through. He stood up and asked "Is he still in here? What he got on?" Janet shook her head and told him that she was sure that he had left out. Now it made sense as to why she was having those dreams. How did he find her? She did well at covering her tracks. She was tired of running but maybe her time had come to an end and it was time to move on.

Davina didn't like the fact that Janet was upset. "Janet, do you want to come live with us for a little while?" Janet was thankful for her newfound family, but she didn't want to be a burden to anyone. "No, I will be fine. Thank you for the offer though."

Robert didn't like the fact that this guy had found her. He thought maybe it was just a coincidence and maybe he was just passing through. Robert was determined to make sure Janet stayed safe. She gave him his wife back and besides she was family. He made a mental note to talk to the family, as well as Mary B and William about what was going on. Robert tried to lighten the mood with some jokes. Unfortunately, it didn't seem to help. Janet kept spacing out. After about thirty minutes or so, they decided to leave to head home. That night Janet stayed with Robert and Davina.

CHAPTER NINE

JEAN AND TIM WERE GETTING RAVEN SETTLED IN AT home. It was crazy because all the children fussed over her. Everyone knew that Miles was her keeper though. When he wasn't in school, he was holding her or feeding her, or just looking at her. Jean would often ask him if he was okay with having a little sister. He would always respond the same, "God told me I have to always be here for her more than the others." Jean never questioned what he meant by that because she was sure he would tell her. Raven would smile big when Miles was around her. He read to her, he talked to her, and he watched her when she slept. Their family was complete. For the first time in a while, there was a sense of calm that had descended over their family.

Everyone was getting along; there were no worries about Bianca or Lucas coming for Kim. Jean couldn't help but worry that there was always calm before the storm. She prayed that storm never came.

Mary B loved the fact that her family was growing. She liked the new additions. She couldn't have picked better mates for her children if she had done it herself. Mary B wanted to get to know more about Janet. There was so much lost time to make up for. She decided to call Janet and ask if she wanted to hang out with an old woman and go shopping. Janet accepted the offer.

The two women became fast friends during the trip, discovering they had a lot in common. Mary B saw strength in this woman. Her life wasn't easy, but she took the bad and pulled happiness out. Janet had been dealt a bad hand in life, as was Mary B. But both had taken the lemons life had thrown at them and created the sweetest lemonade. Janet told Mary B all about her mom, at least what she remembered. That made Mary B happy. She had a part of a sister still here and for that she was thankful.

Janet confided in her aunt about bumping into her ex when they had gone out for dinner. She told her that she was still scared of him. This man had tried to kill her several times. Bo was a monster. In the beginning he was amazingly kind and sweet but that changed in a blink of an eye. Mary B wanted to assure her more than anything that nothing bad was going to happen to her again, but she knew she couldn't promise that. That didn't stop her from praying for favor from God in the matter. She asked Janet if she would consider moving in with her and William, however she declined.

Janet told her that she might leave town for a little while but promised she would be back before too long. She didn't want any of her family in danger because of her ex. Janet admitted to herself that it wasn't so easy to leave this place, she had family now, and they genuinely cared about her and what happened to her. That still amazed her after these last few months.

DAVINA HAD BEEN LOOKING FOR A NEW HOUSE WHILE she was doing her physical therapy. She had hinted to Robert that she had wanted to move. She loved the closeness of having family nearby, but she found a house a few hours away. Robert had made the mistake of promising her anything when she couldn't walk, if she walked again.

The house she found was amazing, it reminded her of the house she grew up in, when it was just, she and her mom, back when things were good. Simple, yet good. She was sure that Robert would not say no, she already made an offer on the home. The realtor was excited for them to come and view the house. In all the years she was in the industry she hadn't encountered many people who made offers on a house sight unseen. Now Davina just had to figure out how to get him there.

When he came home that evening, she told him that she had a doctor's appointment in Richmond, it was her final one and they were going to give her the final okay that all was well. With a happy ending like that of course Robert was on board. Davina's last stipulation was that they bring the children with them. She explained to Robert that way they wouldn't have to rush back home. They could enjoy themselves, without her being in a wheelchair. She knew more than anything that would tug at his heartstrings. Davina knew when to play the guilt card and she played it well.

The appointment was scheduled for two days later. Davina was determined to get the house. The next day the realtor called and told her that the owner had accepted her offer. Davina expressed that she was ready to move in as soon as possible. She was eager to put the past behind her family and start anew just in time for the holidays. Davina felt in her heart that giving them a fresh start would be good for Robert as well. Davina prayed that Robert would be okay with this whole process. She had gone too far to go back now. Talk about walking out on faith. All that was needed was the final okay from Robert.

Robert could tell his wife was up to something, he just couldn't put his finger on it. The truth of the matter was as long as she was happy, then he was happy. They hadn't spent much time out and about since Davina's accident, so if this is what she wanted so be it. He was determined to make sure she was happy. She fought hard to walk again, and she deserved the world. He knew she could have given up a thousand times along the way and he admitted he thought she had a few times, but she always managed to surprise him.

He was excited about this trip to the doctor's office tomorrow, probably more excited than Davina. Robert wanted more than anything for his wife to be whole again. He wanted for her to feel whole again. This would be a step closer to getting their lives back on track.

The next morning, he was already up and ready to go with the children dressed and eating breakfast before Davina woke up. He made Davina's favorite breakfast, which also happened to be the children's favorite too. Robert made French toast with scrambled eggs with cheese and some grits. On the side was some fruit. He had to admit that he loved it too. Davina noticed that he was super excited; she began feeling a bit bad for deceiving him. She prayed that he would forgive her for her going behind his back, but she felt strongly that this was where fate was leading them.

This was nothing against the family, but she had too many bad memories there and she didn't want Robert to be tempted either. Robert had worked hard to stay clean but there was always the thought that life might be too much and he would start using drugs again to cope.

Davina wasn't crazy she did talk to Mary B and Jean about this but swore them to secrecy. She wanted them to know why she felt so strongly about needing the change of scenery. The two women closest to her husband both said they understood and wanted nothing but their happiness. Jean chimed in, "That will give us somewhere to go to visit that's not too far."

Mary B and Jean had seen the pictures of the house online and the asking price and told her she would be crazy not to jump on it. She was only following the advice of the other two important women in his life. He couldn't be mad at that, at least she hoped.

On the drive there, Robert was talking up a storm, he touched on everything from the twins to what he was doing at work, and then finally to the doctor she was supposed to see today. "Where did this doctor come from Vina? Have we met with them before?"

Davina had to be quick with formulating a cover story, "This is the specialist that my doctor was consulting with during my surgeries, and she helped get the therapy plan together. She just wants to make sure things look good. My situation was not your average case and for me to be walking now, is nothing short of a miracle." Robert agreed that made sense.

As they neared the address that Davina had given him, he noticed there were no businesses on the street. He looked at the address on the paper and verified that he had the address right. "Hey babe, is this the correct address? There are just houses here."

Davina hadn't thought about this problem. "Maybe they have a home office babe? Just pull into the house that matches the address. We will just go in and see. There it is right there. There is a car in the driveway, just pull behind it." The house was just as beautiful as the pictures Davina had seen. She hoped she would be able to pull this off.

Once Robert pulled in the driveway Davina hurried out of the car, she began unbuckling Kaloni. She started toward the door, and Robert called out, "Don't you want to make sure this is the right place before we take the children in?"

"It's okay Robert, this is the right place, I'm almost sure of it. Can you unbuckle Kevin?" When she knocked on the door Trish answered and ushered her in quickly. Davina quickly explained that Robert didn't know she had already made an offer to purchase the home, and he thought it was a doctor's office. She asked Trish if she could give her five minutes alone with Robert. Trish agreed, she needed this sale, plus she didn't want to look crazy for accepting an offer from someone who hadn't toured the house.

Finally, Robert knocked on the door and Davina quickly answered it with "Welcome home baby." Robert looked confused for a moment. As he walked into the house, he looked around in awe. This house was beautiful, not huge but it appeared to be pretty spacious. He thought the doctor was smart to put an office here, so they wouldn't have to leave the house for work. That would definitely save on gas money.

"Davina, where is the doctor? I'm ready for some good news." Davina grabbed his hand and walked him around the house.

"Robert, what do you think about this house?"

"I think it is pretty nice. Why do you ask Vina?" Davina was nervous but she knew she had to just come clean and tell him. "I bought this house for you, well for us. Remember I told you I wanted to move, and you promised that I could have anything that I wanted. Do you remember telling me that?" Robert's mouth dropped, he wanted to be furious with his wife, but he could not do it. She was right he had made that promise. He just didn't think it would lead to them moving away from his mom and sister.

"What do you mean exactly when you say that you bought this house? You've been home every day, when did you come and see it? When did you pay for it? How did you pay for it?" Davina knew he would be inquisitive, but she wasn't quite prepared for his rapid-fire barrage of questions.

"Just trust me, the house is ours. I just need to sign on the dotted line. You don't have to put your name on it if you don't want to. I just think this is a good move for us, getting a fresh start and put the past behind us. I'm so sorry for being deceptive by saying I had a doctor's appointment, but I needed to make sure I could get you here. I wanted the kids here to see it too. Everything is taken care of; I just need you to be okay with it. Say something please, even if it's something I don't want to hear."

Robert had been taking in everything his wife had said

and done. "What about my job? What about my parents, and my sister?"

Davina knew that he would be concerned about them. She pulled out her phone and dialed Jean's number and she handed Robert the phone. Before he could get a word out, Jean was rattling off questions. "So how do you like it? I hope you told her that she was amazing. Mom and I are okay with you moving, brother. You have given us a lot of your life especially since I've been back, but you have to live your life also. We want you to be happy. And this way you're hosting New Year's Eve this time. That gives you a few months to get settled and then we are coming to crash."

Robert felt better after talking, well more like listening to his sister, as he couldn't get a word in edgewise. "Davina the house is great, but there is no way that I'm having a 2 hour commute each day for work. That's just crazy."

"You are right. Luckily for you having an awesome wife, you have a few options. The mortgage is covered for about two years. You can drive back home every weekend until you find a job here or you can just start looking for something here. We will be moved in as soon as the closing is done if you agree. The owner is an motivated seller, so that is a plus for us If you're going to stay there during the week at our place or with your mom, then I need to know so I can make sure the movers leave what you may need. I've already cleared it with the landlord, we can pay monthly there if you want to stay."

"You have really thought of everything. You are awesome, and as much as I want to be upset, I really can't be. Even the children appear to be happy with the house. I love my family, but I think it is good for us to be away and we can

start over. This last year has been very trying for us all."
Robert walked over and pulled her in for a hug and as she
tilted her head up to him, he kissed her lips full. "I love you
so much." True indeed the twins were exploring the house.

At that moment Trish poked her head in from the back-
yard. "Hello, is it safe to come in? I didn't hear any yelling."
Davina nodded and spoke up. "Yes, by all means Trish, this
is my husband Robert, and our children, Kevin and Kaloni.
We were just admiring our new home. Isn't that right babe?"
Robert knew when he was beaten, he simply smiled and
nodded yes.

Davina let out a sigh of relief; she knew it could have all
backfired on her. Her husband could be very stubborn when
he wanted to be. Thankfully, this was not one of those times,
and she knew she had used his words against him. She
played dirty and she knew it but it was for a great cause. She
was sure this move was for the best. "Shall we sign some
paperwork and make it official then?" They both nodded yes.

After signing the paperwork, neither Robert nor
Davina were in a rush to leave their new home. If they
would have had furniture there, they probably would have
stayed the night. Reluctantly they headed back home;
Robert had a few words for his mom and sister. He
couldn't believe that they had all colluded behind his back
and he hadn't had a clue. Robert knew he was going to
miss being that close to his family. It was all he knew; he
wouldn't be able to get to them quickly in case something
happened. That was the only drawback about the whole
thing. His family was fragile, there was always something
going on, he wouldn't be able to be right there in the thick
of it. Robert also knew his mom would tell him to live his

life. He would still be in the mix, just not a few miles away.

Robert was determined that the distance wouldn't change things. His family meant the world to him and he wouldn't lose out on that just because he was a few hours away. He looked over at Davina, who had fallen asleep on the drive back, and he thought he couldn't have loved her more than at that moment. Just then Davina stirred and looked up at him. "Why are you looking at me, when you should be focused on the road?"

"You are amazing that's all. I want to ask, but then again, I don't. I'm almost scared to know the answer. Can I ask you where the money come from to buy the house?" Robert reached over and interlaced his fingers with Davina's.

Davina knew he would eventually ask the question. "It's from Joshua and my mom actually. He had an account set up for me a few days after he took me in. He started it with money that Mom had left me, which wasn't a lot, but it helped. He didn't want me to ever have to worry about anything. I left the money there and it earned a lot of interest over the years, so I used the interest to put the down payment down and it will cover the mortgage for at least the first two years. I never told you about it because it didn't matter, and I had forgotten all about it to be honest. When I started looking for a house, something told me to check the account. I did and that was what I found. The original money is still there. It's our nest egg. I didn't want you to want me because of my little bit of money."

Robert smiled to himself. He wanted to strangle her at that moment in time. When he was working hard trying to make sure that they were taken care of, he didn't have to. He thought back to when he started using, that could have been avoided too, but he did understand why she didn't say anything.

"I know you probably want to kill me, but I wanted to be sure that we were going to be okay. I wanted to make sure that you were the man I needed. And you have proven that time and time again. I wanted to show you, that I appreciate you and all that you do. I am your ride or die chick, I have your back because you've had mine for so long now." Robert loved this woman more than life itself; he would never have expected that from her.

No one other than his family had ever shown him that type of unconditional love. "Thank you," was all he could get past his lips at that time.

"You are more than welcome. I saw the house and immediately thought it would be perfect for our family, so I did this for us. I want us to have a fresh start. There are a lot of memories not all bad but not all good either back home. I hope you understand why I did this. I just love you and want you to not feel like you have to do this all alone. You are not in this alone, that I promise you. I'm sorry if I ever made you feel that way." Davina just didn't know that she was in for it when they got home.

Robert had been a patient man, but he needed his wife in a way he didn't think possible. He gave Vina that look that made her insides flare with heat, and she nodded. Good thing they were only a mile or so from home, had they not been, Robert surely would have gotten a ticket. This was the beginning of their new life.

Davina called Joshua the next afternoon to tell him that she was moving. She wanted to tell him what she had done with the money just in case he was watching it. She knew all too well that he didn't play around when it came to money. In his life he had made more money than he could ever spend, so he donated a lot to various charities. When he wasn't working, he was investing, and had done well at it.

Little did Davina know, but he had started accounts for the twins just as he done with her, they were set for life. Joshua told her that he was proud of her and wanted nothing but the best for her. In the beginning he hadn't approved of Davina and Robert's relationship, he didn't believe that Robert could adequately provide for her. Robert over the years had proved them both wrong. He showed them that he was the man for her. Joshua made Davina promise as soon as she felt up to it, that she should go ahead and look for a space for her a boutique. He remembered that she used to make clothes and she was pretty good at it. She fought him tooth and nail because he wanted her to go into the medical field. He wanted to see her fulfill that part of her dream before he left this world. The same way she played the guilt card on Robert, Joshua knew how to play it on her. Davina could only smile as she hung up the phone; she loved that man as if he was her own father.

CHAPTER TEN

JANET TOOK SOME TIME OFF FROM WORK, ALTHOUGH SHE hated to do so. The success that Davina had with her recovery did wonders for Janet's reputation. The hospital wanted her on staff with them, which meant she would have to leave the practice she was working for. She would be able to work her own schedule, and she would have a never-ending supply of clients.

Janet told them she needed a little bit of time and wanted to give the appropriate notice to her current employer. She should have been jumping for joy at the offer she just received from the hospital, but it was hard to be excited and in fear of your life at the same time. Janet had been spending a lot of time at the gun range since she had some free time now. Her aim was on point and she was ready to protect herself should the occasion arise. She decided not to leave the home she had started making here.

Janet hadn't seen Bo around since that night that she ran into him. She was not totally confident that he was gone. His card was still in her coat pocket, she looked to see if it had an address listed, and it did not. She wasn't convinced of anything other than she needed to stay vigilant.

She flashed back to one day when she had come home from work a few hours late. Rushing trying to get things handled, she neglected to call him and let him know. This was in the early stages before she realized just how deep his jealousy flowed. When she arrived home, she had already taken off her work clothes because her client had an accident, and some had gotten on her. She used the shower at the office like she had many times before, and she thought nothing of it. She always was prepared with a second set of clothes in the trunk of her car, because in her line of work, you never knew what would or could happen. The body wash that she had in her workbag was a different scent then the one she used at home; again, she didn't think it was an issue.

She didn't even get in the door good, before Bo was on her. She didn't know what was happening, all she remembered was that he had her jacked up against the wall by her throat. Janet couldn't believe it, but Bo was sniffing her out like a dog.

"What are you doing? What did I do? Why in the world are you smelling me?" He just kept smelling her.

"Where have you been? Who have you been with? Those are not the clothes you had on when you left this morning. Why did you take a shower?" Bo was intense with his questions. Janet could see the anger in the rigidness of his face.

Janet was scared out of her mind. This was the second time that he had jumped on her for no reason. "If you calm down, I can explain. Mrs. Johansen had an accident, some got on my pants. You know I can't deal with any nastiness on me. So, I did what I always have done and that is I took a shower and changed clothes."

Bo started to relax a little, his breathing started returning to normal. "Why didn't you just call me Janet? I was waiting here for you, and I was starting to worry. You know that I can't imagine anyone else with you. The thought of you with someone else drives me crazy. I'm sorry if I hurt you, you know I would never hurt you on purpose. I love you baby. Please say you will forgive me?"

One of the worst mistakes of her life was forgiving him and saying it was okay. She should have run for the hills, and if she had known that it was only the beginning she would have. She loved him though and thought he loved her too. She just didn't know that his definition of love was until death, literally.

Bo was indeed still in town. He kept his distance from Janet; he didn't want to scare her. He made it his business to learn her schedule, and he was content just watching her for the time being. He knew enough to know she wasn't dating anyone; she did go to the gun range a lot. She was spending a lot of time with that chick he seen her with that night at the restaurant.

He remembered their life a little differently than Janet. Bo had been super aggressive, but it didn't start out that way. When the two of them met, he was immediately taken by her. Janet had a smile to die for. He showed her that he was a good man by constantly showering her with his affection and gifts. Bo would always bring her flowers to her job, or to her client's house it didn't matter where she was, he wanted to make sure she knew he loved her.

Bo grew up with a dad who was in and out of jail, so he barely knew him. He just knew enough to know he didn't want to be anything like him. The sad thing was, he was more like him then he could have ever imagined.

Bo never meant to hurt Janet. He loved her and he just got upset when he thought someone else wanted her. He kept telling himself that he needed to get help, but it wasn't until he nearly killed her the last time, that he realized he had gone too far. He was out of control and he lost the one person he knew he could count on. Bo wanted Janet back and he felt that he could get her to take him back, but it was going to require patience. That was not his best quality, but he was determined to get her back or die trying.

AFTERWORD

Thank You for Reading....

Don't forget to sign up for
Mind Flow Publishing & Production LLC's Newsletter @
www.mindflowpublishingproduction.com

Email us for autographed or additional paperback copies @
mindflowpubpro@gmail.com

Other Titles Also Available Include

Mental Interlude --- Poetry
The Mary B Chronicles 1 & 2 --- Fiction
Journey to Living (Kindle Only) --- Inspirational
Simple Complexity --- Poetry
Spoken From The Heart --- Poetry
Dreams Do Come True (Kindle Only) --- Fiction
Charisma's Homecoming --- Fiction

For Her Love --- Fiction

Available Through
Amazon
Barnes & Noble
Kindle

Coming Soon

Freedom In The Cage Series --- Fiction
A Love For Holly --- Cozy Romance
A Prince For Me --- Romantic Comedy

UPCOMING TITLES

Upcoming Titles Will Be Available
Through
Amazon
Barnes & Noble
Kindle
Apple iBooks
Kobo

ABOUT THE AUTHOR

Although I'm still considered new to the publishing world, I have hit the ground running full speed ahead. In my first year, I was signed to Mind Flow Publishing & Production LLC, and I have published a total of 6 books. I have earned Amazon's Best Sellers Top 100 orange banner. My works are spread across several genres such as; Poetry, Inspirational, Urban Fiction and Christian Fiction. I will be trying my hand at cozy mysteries, romance, and sci-fi. My love for writing started when I was about 12, writing poetry and writing speeches for various oratorical contests. Inspiration for my craft is pulled from my own life experiences, as well as others. I have been featured on several podcasts, as well as Up and Coming Authors Newsletters. When I'm not writing, I love to design shadowboxes, and create personalized greeting cards. I have released my 3rd poetry book (Spoken from the Heart) in August 2019. Current books available are The Mary B Chronicles 1 & 2, Mental Interlude, and Journey to Living, Simple Complexity, and Dreams Do Come True, Spoken from the Heart, and Charisma's Homecoming. All of which are available on Amazon, and www. mindflowpublishingproduction.com.